PENGUIN BOOKS

WILD EAST

PENGUIN BOOKS

UK | USA | Canada | Ireland | Australia
India | New Zealand | South Africa

Penguin Books is part of the Penguin Random House group of companies
whose addresses can be found at global.penguinrandomhouse.com.

www.penguin.co.uk
www.puffin.co.uk
www.ladybird.co.uk

Penguin
Random House
UK

First published 2024

001

Text design by Mandy Norman
Printed in Great Britain by Clays Ltd, Elcograf S.p.A.

The authorized representative in the EEA is Penguin Random House Ireland,
Morrison Chambers, 32 Nassau Street, Dublin D02 YH68

A CIP catalogue record for this book is available from the British Library

ISBN: 978-0-241-64544-4

All correspondence to:
Penguin Books
Penguin Random House Children's
One Embassy Gardens, 8 Viaduct Gardens, London SW11 7BW

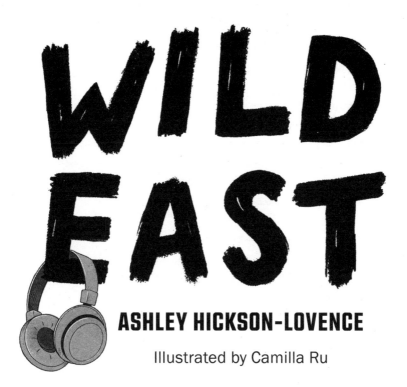

WILD EAST

ASHLEY HICKSON-LOVENCE

Illustrated by Camilla Ru

PENGUIN

CONTENT WARNING

Before you begin reading, please be aware that small parts of this book may be triggering for some readers. While it is a work of fiction, this book is grounded in many aspects of modern life and covers some serious topics that readers should be aware of, including knife crime, county lines and physical violence.

AUTHOR'S NOTE

Growing up with my mum and little brother in our council flat in Hackney, East London, I never thought I would be an author or a doctor of Creative Writing with a PhD one day. Mainly because, when I was at school, I rarely read books written by people like me, about people like me.

Slowly things seem to be changing.

If you've ever felt unseen, unsure or unsafe, a little shy or even outright terrified, in or out of the classroom, then *Wild East* has been written for you. This is a story for those who – like the main character, Ronny – might not consider themselves readers usually but are still, in some way, in some form, a lover of words.

Ashley Hickson-Lovence

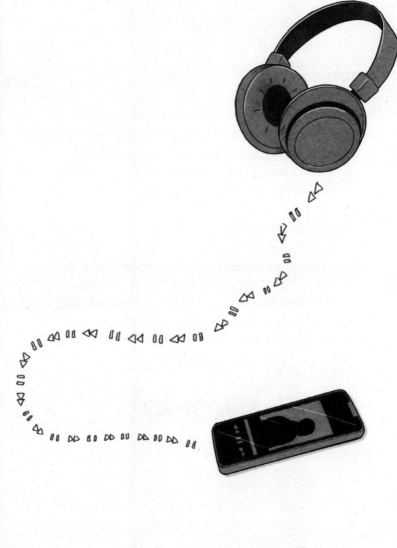

WILD EAST PLAYLIST

**Plants don't grow
when it's dark and cold.
Something that seemed so simple
is the part unknown.**

– Frankie Stew and Harvey Gunn

PROLOGUE

**A glance as sharp
as a shard of broken glass.**

His dark eyes slicing souls open
with crystal-clear precision
on the top deck of this 43 bus,
we've become targets locked in his vision.

'What you looking at?' he says,
words all jagged and pointy,
loaded like a strap and hanging heavy,
weighty enough for every
passenger to hear.

We didn't know we were
looking at him, not really,
Maz and I, no more than a
little peep if we were – certainly
didn't mean to cause offence.
We've just been chilling, in all honesty,
chatting and joking around
doing stupid impressions
of our teachers and stuff –
but this guy sat at the very back
is getting all riled up.

'Oi, did you not hear me?'
he says louder than before,
his voice all strained and spiky.
'What **you** looking at?'
He seems to be addressing **me**
now only.

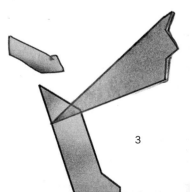

3

He's sat with this other guy,
quieter but looks just as menacing,
both like sixteen, seventeen,
eighteen at a stretch maybe.
Either way, just a few years older than us
and unlike Maz and me,
not in school uniform.

I think they've got it twisted
because I know I've never seen
either of them before.
Where I come from, you remember
every spot, scratch or scar
of someone's face, so this must be a case
of mistaken identity, it has to be.

The two of them sit sprawled across
the five seats at the back and we're sat
half turned to them,
Maz on one side of the aisle,
me on the other,
just a few rows in front,
on the top deck of this double-decker bus,
the current scene of this unprovoked
but not totally unexpected verbal attack.
When you live in London you can't ever
let your guard down just like that.

Me and Maz, best friends since Year Seven,
same form class, school football team,
always get this bus home together,

take it basically every day,
from our school in Archway,
past Holloway,
and Highbury, along City Road,
through Islington and into Hackney.

Maz is mad good at art,
wants to do it for GCSE.
He's a guaranteed Grade 9, easily
one of the best in the year,
maybe even the whole school;
good at doing realistic portraits of people
and landscapes of the city.

**But this picture here
is not looking pretty.**

In seconds the mood has shifted.
This guy's serious and now the blood's
proper thumping under my skin,
as painful as punches to the ribs.
He's angrily pointing his fingers at me
and his fury is hard to ignore,
we're definitely looking at him now
even if we weren't looking before.

'Nothing to say, yeah,' he says,
again, just speaking to me specifically.
'Not a big man any more, yeah,' he adds,
rising from his seat now, aggressively.

We can't take this, can we?

Maz has had enough and
starts to speak up,
taking matters into his
own hands on my behalf.
Calls him names in reply,
names he deserves undoubtedly
but still feels strange to hear at like four
in the afternoon on a Wednesday.

But I suppose he's
got the right idea –
we can't look weak,
made to look a joke
by this joker talking silly
in front of all these people,
just like ten minutes or so from our ends
where we grew up,
where we were born and raised.

The other passengers seem to ignore
what's going on completely,
or what might be
just about to happen.
They only half look,
they only half care,
this disagreement a minor inconvenience
they can forget about in five or ten minutes.

Some of them saw Stormzy
the other summer, headlining Glastonbury
so instead of getting involved,
defend or protect,
they read a *Guardian* book review
or scroll through ASOS
for something to wear
for their work summer barbecue.

This is the youth of today,
and this is what they do:
through anger is how they communicate.

Blame the Mayor of London, Sadiq Khan.
Blame drill music.
Blame bad parenting.

(They don't care. Not really.)

'I'm not doing this. Come, Ronny,'
suggests Maz sensibly
as he gets up and
heads towards the stairs quickly,
ready to get off before all hell breaks loose,
before this all gets out of hand.

The passengers breathe a sigh of relief,
can get on with the rest of their day and maybe
that's the end of it. This drama to them
like a scene from *Top Boy* on Netflix,
watch a bit and then press the OFF switch.

But as we stomp down the stairs,
Maz spouting parting shots,
me staying quiet,
scampering behind trying to keep up
without looking back,
I hear footsteps **follow us off**.

Now we're walking towards Islington Green,
and even Maz seems keen to get away,
but this guy is not giving me the space,
his trigger finger
jabbing my temple and I'm
too shook to react,
too scared to respond.
My heart in my throat,
the heat in my face.

These guys are moving mad,
the main one in particular,
limbs flailing and fizzy,
legs and arms all frenetic.

In our rush to escape and get away,
we barge past a posh couple
who at first act outraged
but then see what's going on
and say nothing.

She's brunette and wearing Birkenstocks,
he's wearing khaki shorts
and camo-coloured Crocs.

I spot the tightness of his knuckles as he
grips her hand and
leads her from the commotion.
I clock his watch – could be
a Rolly, or an Audemars –
and he's brave for wearing
one of those around these parts,
but at this moment,
he's not the one in danger . . .

We are.

Because this bus guy's
bobbing about like a boxer,
but it's not his fists he's threatening us with.
No, there's too much fury involved now,
he's in too deep to back out
and seems ready to match words
with actual action.

There's something shapely in this boy's tracksuit,
recognizable from playground stories
or films, music videos on YouTube.

The sunlight is gleaming off
his shiny forehead,
droplets of his sweat spread
and start to drip as this scuffle spills
from the pavement on to the streets
and Maz is shouting back now,
not letting it go –

it's not what he knows –
but when the guy's hand dips,
I duck.

Me and Maz, best friends since Year Seven;
same form class, school football team,
but he's in real trouble here because
now it's two against one.

I've gone.

I'm fleeing the scene at speed
and, as I break into a
full sprint and glance back,
I see a glimmer of a knife-edge,
the stainless-steel shine
of a black-handled seven-inch.

Maz – weaponless, of course,
his only defence his desperate pleas –
is floored.

The liquid pours:
his blood, my tears.

AUGUST

**Mistaken identity . . .
one of the main reasons for the move.**

After what happened to Maz,
Mum got it into her head
that if we didn't leave London soon,
she was going to find me dead
just yards from our front door,
having been wrongly targeted
by some
hot-headed,
knife-wielding
gang-member goon.

She's been going on about it for months,
shouting at me to **Hurry up and come watch
Riz Lateef!** (which is pretty insensitive
after what happened, if you ask me);
or forcing me to listen to a similar news story
on ITV whenever there's a new incident
involving the death of an innocent teenager.

I love London,
it's where I was born,
it's where I grew up,
it's the only place I really know,
the only place I've ever called home,
but she has a point, I suppose.

Too regularly recently,
young Black boys have been

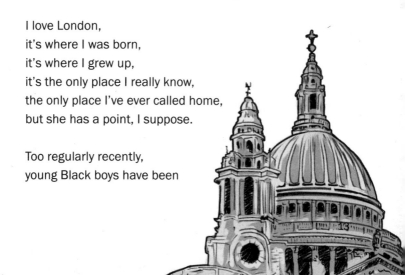

losing their lives
because from afar
they look like someone else.
Their silhouette in the dark
from a distance
resembling someone similar.

It happened to that boy
from Forest Gate,
and that boy from Barking
and a load of others too –
boys who wanted to do
chemistry at university,
or play up front for Chelsea.

Boys who'd never been
in trouble with the police,
simply in the wrong place
at the wrong time;
chased, hounded and hurt by young men
the same age or similar,
on pushbikes, mopeds or
in matte-black Mercedes
too tinted for their own good,
too heavy-handed to think properly.

Innocent and **brilliant** boys like Maz.

'London is bad and getting worse,'
Mum said, as we left the big city
and made our way up the motorway

past an airport that must be Stansted,
according to the giant road signs.

'No place for a young Black boy
who will go to
Oxford or Cambridge one day.'
She winks, nudging my
right shoulder with her left.

Not again, I think,
rolling my eyes, avoiding her gaze.
For me it's far too early
to be thinking about
Oxford or Cambridge just yet –
or any university, if I'm lucky
enough to even get into one.
I'm only just about to start Year Ten.

There's no point arguing any more though,
as much as I've tried to push back recently.

I might be far from convinced by this move
but now this very van is crammed
with literally everything we own,
and I'm about two hours away from a place
I've only ever heard of playing FIFA,
or when the football team are sitting
rock-bottom of the Premier League.

Nope, I've never even been
to Norwich before.

Don't know anyone who has, personally.
When I looked it up
on my phone the other day,
it was basically in its own little corner,
not wanting to get in the way.
I had to slide my finger
along my iPhone screen
more times than I thought,
just to find it.

We've only rented the van for one night
so Kemi is driving us up
with all our stuff,
and then driving back down to London
tonight on his own.

He's technically my mum's ex,
but they still get along
and he's always been there
through the years
to offer a helping hand –
like a stepdad to me of sorts,
you could say.

The three of us are squashed in at the front.
Me on the left and Mum in the middle.
Kemi's on the right-hand side,
driving with both hands gripped on the wheel
and squinting through his
frameless thick-lensed glasses
at the satnav on his phone,

probably thinking that this journey
is actually much longer than he
thought it was gonna be.

Mum offered to pay him for driving us
all the way there and helping us unload,
but he just said a KFC
at a service station somewhere will do.
So after a quick munch at a place
called Birchanger Green,
we're back on the road.

It's been over an hour and a half already
and still no sign of any city in sight.
Just endless fields diminishing
in the ever-dimming light.

I write a few lines on my Notes app.
Too early to call them lyrics yet,
just ideas, sentences, fragments, puzzle pieces.
Things to come back to later maybe,
turn them into some kind of song.

> **leaving the ends**
> **doing seventy on the motorway**
> **with stacks at the back**
> **not money but boxes**

Sounds a bit bait but music is more
important to me than the air I breathe.
I can't even brush my teeth without

a song playing in the background.
I'm obsessed by rhythm, and beat,
the lyrics and the delivery.
Basically every day,
I've got some snippet of some song
stuck in my head.

Kemi's selection of music is decent:
old-school funky house and catchy garage vibes
but I put my headphones on anyway,
which are always either on my head
or wrapped round my neck, and
put my favourite playlist on shuffle.
It's made up of artists like
Dave, Bawo, Headie One, Central Cee,
Frankie Stew and Harvey Gunn
and some drill artists too.

Kano plays, 'Class of Deja'
from his album *Hoodies all Summer*,
a song I heard live just last week.

Well, sort of.

I didn't actually go to All Points East,
the tickets were like £80 I think
but I loitered as close as I could get
to the entrance of the park when he was on.

I stayed until the very end
as people started
flooding out in their thousands.
Bleary-eyed and barely able
to walk, or really talk,
but just about able to get out,
through slurred words,
that they wanted to go to some place
called *The Dolphin*, and babbling
on about wanting
to see Bicep in Barcelona one day.

Another roundabout.

Modified road sign: **Thetford oranges**

Giant tank-shaped sign: **COMBAT PAINTBALL**

It's getting darker and darker
and still no streetlights, only
tiny red lane lights on the road
that Kemi tells me are called 'cat's eyes'.

There aren't even many cars ahead to
help guide us, so Kemi is
concentrating proper hard
just to make sure we get there in one piece.

The names of the towns sound so strange:
Attleborough, Wymondham, Swaffham.
I'm definitely not in London any more.

Eventually we arrive into Norwich.
'**A Fine City**', the sign says.

We turn into our new street,
with the orange light from the lamp-posts
illuminating the houses of
this quite posh-looking residential road.

I've only ever seen
pictures of our new home on Rightmove,
but first impressions in person are good.
Unlike the flat we had back in Hackney,
this is a whole house,
with black and blue
wheelie bins instead of rubbish chutes,
three bedrooms, two bathrooms
and a front and back garden.

It's late by the time we arrive but
Kemi and Mum and me
carry the boxes from the back of the van
into our new home.

As we unload our stuff,
bits of furniture
and bin bags full of our clothes,
a man from next door –
our new neighbour probably,
who we've clocked spying already,
watching us suspiciously
from behind his curtains –

shuffles closer in his dingy
flip-flops and offers to help.
White, mid-forties and balding,
Puma jogging bottoms and a plain blue polo.

Mum politely declines but he insists
and, as if worried he might catch something,
cautiously grabs two black bags
from the back of the van.

'So, where've you all come from then?'
he asks, as he dumps some
of our belongings down
on a free space along the wall
of our new living room.

'East London, Hackney,'
Mum says as she
steps in with a spider plant
in one hand and a small side table in the other,
squeezing past our new beer-bellied neighbour,
who stands right in the middle of the doorway
with his chunky hands on his chunky hips.

'Oh yeah, and before then?'

'Palmers Green,' Mum replies firmly,
unable to hide an obvious hint of hostility.

Even though it's gone ten and already
feels a few degrees colder here than in London,

I'm starting to sweat as I carry
a set of four dining chairs
from the van into the middle room.

'You know what, son,'
our new neighbour starts saying,
'you look a lot like that footballer . . .
what's-his-face that fought for them
school dinners during the holidays.
Plays for Man United? Missed that big penalty
at Wembley the other year against Italy . . .
Marcus Rashford, that's it.'

There is a long, uncomfortable pause as
Kemi and Mum stare at him sternly.

'Ah, is it?' I say awkwardly,
as I put down the chairs
and give an unconvincing half smile.

It's been twenty minutes or so but
we have a case of **mistaken identity**
already, in my **new home city**.

SEPTEMBER

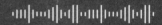

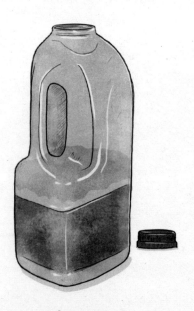

I was gonna have Shreddies for breakfast
this morning, but it was only
when I went to pour the milk
that I noticed that the little
that was left was off.

The insides had separated,
gone all thick and clumpy at the top
with water-like liquid at the bottom.
So I just left for my first day
at my new school,
belly still rumbling.

Last night before she left for work,
Mum did ask me to
get some from the shop,
but because of the nerves I felt
starting school today,
I just totally forgot.

I decide to walk to my new school
instead of taking the bus,
because I haven't worked out
what route I need to get yet.

And I've drained all my data
for the month already
but I took a couple of screenshots
of the directions last week.

I've downloaded some of
my favourite Spotify playlists too,
so I can still listen to
some of my favourite songs if I want to.

As I walk to school,
I go back to a song
on my phone
I've been writing from before,
and add a bit more:

> **leaving the ends for country**
> **but not shotting pebbs**
> **like them roadmen do**

I'm always writing down lines
for some song I'm working on.
Things I see, feel or
experience day to day –
everything from
grief to ambition to hunger.

I walk down a long road
that starts from a roundabout
with a drive-thru McDonald's on the corner.
I would buy a hash brown or bacon roll,
but I want to save
the little bit of change I have for now,
as I get to grips living in this new city.

Growing up and not having much money,
any little you do have,
you learn to use wisely.

I reach a small village
that looks all classy and posh,
full of mums pushing prams:
Birkenstocks and Ray-Bans.

Then I turn right
and I'm looking at the school gates.

I've arrived proper early, there's still
ages until the start of registration,
so I decide to walk around a bit,
try and burn off some anxious energy.
Take in my new surroundings,
get to know the place a little.

The school looks different from London ones –
more spread out, has more space,
takes up more ground,
with lots of separate buildings,
like a university would look, I imagine,
with different blocks dotted all around.

As the minutes pass,
more students start to arrive
and my stomach proper hurts
from the nerves.

Students reunite, multiply,
chatting and catching up
after not seeing each other
since before the summer holidays.

A group that started off small gets
bigger and **bigger** and **bigger**,
louder and **louder**.

But I'm alone,
so I find a little bench by the tennis courts,
take out my phone,
open the Notes app
and start writing some more lines,
adding to what I've got so far . . .

CHANGES

**leaving the ends for country
but not a roadman shotting pebbs,
an estate where I come from
means high-rise tower blocks
not proper houses with three beds**

**moving to this new city
full of pubs for pint-drinking white men
wearing bootcuts with shoes
and showing off neck tattoos
and random people saying hello to you**

**someone said there's only one Black barber in this city
and the buses are the wrong colour**

just like me to many in my new city

but enough was enough, packed a couple bags
moved out of ends so needed a couple hands
from a council flat to a rented house
moving to new ends from old ones

now I just need to clear my mind,
Stick on 'Humble Pie' and let me vibe
only got small hours until it dries
hang a portrait up, Mona Lisa eyes
it hides all the cracks,
I'm running out of time (trust)

I'm going through some changes
not sure if I'll make it
people come and go but
I'm just doing me on this path I've taken

listen, that's the future
gotta think of now, that's the bigger picture
get a little loud when my mind is triggered
I just hope I get a little richer
writing lines about life,
thinking of the bigger picture

pandemic wasn't the one, times got peak
life isn't fair, the last few years have been deep
hoping next year is the time to dream
trust me time flies
back in May times,

Maz lost his life
never understood or comprehended time
I just need to get it right this time
never thought I'd say this, so it's getting sung
writing all your feelings in a song is tough (trust)
going through some changes, but it's called
growing up

The energy is different here,
that much is clear.
There aren't many other Black students
from what I can see so far.
Or students of colour generally.

The other kids, of all years,
but who largely look the same
in a strange kind of way,
shoot glances at me
from my Afro to my Kickers,
and half smile in my direction, unsure.

I just keep my head down,
try to keep to myself.
Turn up the volume of
Frankie Stew in my headphones
to drown out the first-day anxiety
and put me more at ease.

As late as I can leave it,
I start making my way to reception,
hoping someone might show me

to my new form class
or wherever it is I need to be.

I make it there eventually,
directed by the Head of Year,
who spotted me looking a little lost.
But I'm the last one to walk in, and
everyone just stares at me as I am told by
my form tutor, Ms Stratton,
to take a seat at the back.
My tactic to go unnoticed
backfiring massively.

To make it worse, as I discreetly
fluff out my Afro with my comb
after it's been squashed down a little
from the weight of my headphones,
the boy next to me,
with blond-brown hair and blue-green eyes,
taps my shoulder and says,

'Cool hair, my bro, can I have a feel?'

OCTOBER

I put my headphones on
and play one of my favourites –
Frankie Stew and Harvey Gunn's
'Plants Don't Grow' from their EP
Handle With Care.

There's something deep
about the lyrics I like;
in some ways, the words
kind of remind me of Maz:

> *all the things that I feel I still don't show*
> *I'm working on myself daily heal me slow*
> *and I feel ashamed of myself in a way*
> *I haven't been there for you, you been the same.*
> *I feel so guilty for things I weren't there for*
> *and I think about it most days*

The words hit different, especially
after leaving London for Norwich
and the madness of what happened to Maz.
Sometimes I can't help but think about the past,
things I've lost, moments of doubt,
that crazy uncertainty of
not knowing what the future has in store.

It's Friday and instead of
English this morning
we have some
writing workshop with a local poet,
which, I can't lie, sounds pretty terrible,

35

but my new English teacher, Mr Bruce,
said I should go.

Even though I like writing,
would say I love it, actually,
I don't much rate poetry;
all that Shakespeare stuff
I find kind of complicated,
and trying to remember all the different forms:
sonnets, odes, limericks.
I still don't really know
the difference between them.

When I think about it deeply
there aren't many things in English
I've really proper enjoyed studying.
There haven't been that many
books we've read that I could relate to,
that have spoken to me like music does.
And I never thought I was any
good at English anyway,
because my old teacher at
my old school used to say
that my handwriting was too messy.

I bet I'm only invited to go
to this poetry club thing
because I'm what they call *Pupil Premium*,
basically meaning I come
from a poorer family.
But Mr Bruce says it might help me

write better stories for the descriptive writing bit
of the English Language paper of my GCSEs
and that the session is just for one hour,
every Friday, for the next sixteen weeks.

I'm still not convinced that poetry
is the best use of my time
or the best way to make
any money for me and Mum
when I'm older.

It's only because I get to miss
one English lesson a week
that I decide to give
the first session a go.

One thing I've noticed about
this school so far is that
the girls are either called Eva or Evie.
All the boys are basically called Riley,
Dylan or Harrison.
There's not much variation.
Not like you get in London.
One of the boys in my old form
was called 'Praisethelord'.
No lie. One word. Praisethelord,
as in Praise . . . the . . . Lord.
He was a proper funny guy though.

I walk in with the rest of the group,
not really knowing the others,
not really knowing what to expect.

I take a seat at the back
at an empty table of two,
and thankfully no one joins me.
I'm left alone for a bit to just sit
and suss out the situation.

Although I'm feeling a little doubtful,
I have to say that he looks kinda cool though,
this poet standing at the front of the drama studio.
He wears a baggy oversized denim shirt,
cherry-red Dr. Martens and baggy black jeans.

He welcomes everyone in energetically,
telling us that there is no seating plan
and we can sit anywhere basically,
and tells us his name is Lucas and
that he's a published poet and performer,
as he hands out our new notebooks.

He instructs us to put our names on the front,
then tells us to write down the line:
Guess who I saw in Tesco last night . . .
at the very top of the first page.

He explains at great speed,
almost like he's spitting some song,
that we mustn't take our pens off the paper
for the entire five-minute duration.

'Even if you don't know what to write,
and it feels like you're just scribbling
pure gibberish,' he continues, 'just repeat

the same words over and over again –
Guess who I saw in Tesco last night . . .
Guess who I saw in Tesco last night –
until that spark occurs and something
magic,' he says, pointing to his heart, '*comes alive.*'

This should be easy in theory
cos I'm always writing.
But it's different when you're
forced to think of stuff on the spot
about something as random as
who I might have seen
in the supermarket yesterday,
when I didn't even go to Tesco last night.

The five minutes have begun
and everyone starts scribbling
with their heads down,
focusing really hard like they've just thought
of this proper banging story right from the off,
but I'm stuck, not knowing how to start.

I jot down a few random words
but nothing that good really comes into my mind;
nothing that really makes sense,
nothing that I'm proud of,
and I'm relieved when
the five minutes are up,
after what feels more like ten.

'Well done, guys,' Lucas says.
'It's never easy to just start writing cold like that.

But remember there's never any pressure here.
This is a safe space,' he adds,
'to write whatever you want,
however you want to write it.'

'Right then.' He clasps his
hands together dramatically,
and in the accent of an old
British gangster asks, 'So, who's got
a couple of lines for me then?
Remember, you only have to share if you want to,'
he adds, returning to his normal voice.

A lot of the others put their hands up to share
but I just keep my head
all the way down, hoping not to be seen,
hoping to shrink into my chair
and completely disappear.

It seems to do the job.
With my eyes firmly staring at the floor,
I'm thankfully ignored.

For the next activity,
he gives us this poem to look at
called 'I Come From' by Dean Atta,
who was inspired
by Robert Seatter.

I write down the words
'I come from . . .'

as the title on the second page
of my new notebook,
though I don't really know how to start.

But after a few seconds of thinking-time
and seeing all the other
students scrawling away,
I take a deep breath and give it a go anyway,
trying to muster whatever
motivation and energy
I have inside me:

I COME FROM

I come from stinky thick piss in the lifts
I come from scary shotters in the stairwell
I come from noisy neighbours screaming all night
Turkish to the left and Lithuanian to the right
I come from milk that was often off
I come from greasy delicious kebab meat and 'Chilli sauce, boss?'
I come from not having much money
so having to make what little we have last
I come from boys burning the back of bus seats with 20p lighters
I come from watching the world go by from the top of my block
I come from dreaming into the distance and wanting to escape
I come from waiting for Mum to come home as it
got too late to stay awake –

Just as I'm getting into it,
Lucas exclaims loudly from behind me:
'Wow, Ronny!
Look how much you've written already!'
Pointing excitedly at my notebook.
'It is Ronny, right?'

Without me knowing,
this nosey poet has been
spying my words over my shoulder.
I suddenly feel all violated and embarrassed,
almost like he's just barged in on me
sitting on the toilet or something.

It feels even worse somehow because he
seems to like what I've done,
so I instinctively fold myself over my notebook,
all annoyed, and turn my back to him.

··||·||·||···

In English, Mr Bruce says,
'The lesson today is about similes,'
which makes me roll my eyes because
like a narcoleptic poet
I can write similes in my sleep.

I write down the title
and today's learning objective
but zone in and out of what Sir's saying;
instead I'm just trying to think of a line

that rhymes with the start of a song
I started to write yesterday.

I spend most of the lesson
writing down lyrics
at the back of my exercise book:
rhymes and half rhymes, puns and punchlines,
trying to make it all fit together like
a picture-perfect puzzle.

Trying not to be too precious,
knowing the words won't be
perfect first-time round,
I'm just sort of vomiting the words down,
getting different ideas on the page
to fiddle and tamper with later,
then add it to an instrumental perhaps.
A banging Harvey Gunn one.

They're just little observations really.
Things about school, moving house,
adjusting to this new life in
this strange little city.

As Sir waffles on, I'm in my own world,
imagining me spitting these same words
that I'm jotting down this very minute,
in some fancy big-time producer's studio or
doing a Daily Duppy on GRM Daily
or in front of thousands at Wireless Festival
or Strawberries & Creem.

Everyone has dreams, and mine
is to showcase my way with words to the world.

I posted a snippet of me spitting a few bars
on my Insta stories last week,
just me in my bedroom and
filmed on my phone.

It didn't really blow up
with a lot of views to begin with
but it didn't completely flop
and make me look a fool
on the 'BTEC Grime' IG page,
so I consider that progress.

Everyone has to start somewhere.

I'm just starting to find my flow a little,
make progress with this song,
when Mr Bruce suddenly
decides to move
another student who's been
talking too much apparently,
and has been given several warnings already,
to come and sit next to me.

I move my bag off the seat proper reluctantly,
like passengers on the bus do back in London,
and shuffle across just a bit to make more room.

'My name's Leigh, by the way,'
he says all chirpily.

I look at him, unsure.
If we were adults,
this is where we would
shake hands or something
but instead I give a little nod
and a semi-unfriendly grunt.

'You *can* tell me yours, you know.
I don't bite, well, not on a weekday anyway,'
he says melodramatically,
lowering into his chair without taking his
mischievous-looking eyes off me.

ılı|ıı|ıı

It's a nice day, not that
hot but still kinda sunny,
so I decide to walk the slightly
longer way home from school
through Eaton Park.

The park's not massive
like some of the ones back in London,
but it has football pitches,
tennis courts, a skateboard park and a little café,
even a miniature railway.

The vibe is kind of calm too –
you can feel it in the air,
just normal people enjoying the space,
stretching their legs
and filling their lungs.
Everyone is just out here
trying to catch a last bit of sun
before the nights start drawing in
and winter comes.

Whether you live in
North London or Norwich,
everyone just wants to feel part of a community,
a safe place, within a group,
where they belong,
where they feel appreciated,
like a group of football fans
going to an away game on a Saturday;
or bus drivers chatting away
changing shifts outside the garage;
or driving instructors giving each other that
random wave I've seen them do.

Earlier today, Mr Bruce,
who I'm starting to think is pretty safe actually,
set us a mock paper as GCSE
practice for homework.

'Write a description suggested by the picture.'

It's due tomorrow,
so I open a new note on my
phone and start observing
the world around me
as I walk around my new city.

I write down things I can see,
things I can hear and smell,
to try to keep the writing sensory
and feel 3D so the readers,
(well, Mr Bruce
in particular, obviously),
can **_imagine it clearly_** –
it's something he's always telling me.

I decide to head into the centre
of the city for inspiration.
I've been before, had a little explore,
when I had to get a few new bits for school
a few weeks ago, but I never really took it in,
never really looked around that closely.

I stroll along Unthank Road.

More or less everybody you walk past
says _hello_ or at the very least
smiles at you warmly,
almost like they know you
personally – and even though
I've been here a few weeks now,
that still takes getting used to.

Norwich has been nice enough to me
but the thing is though,
there's not *that* much diversity in the city.

I've only seen a few Black people so far
and deep down inside,
as nice as people here all seem,
it's hard to shake off the feeling that
some people would prefer it if I wasn't here.

I walk through Chapelfield Gardens
where the homeless look harmless, helpless,
so unusually friendly that I would definitely
give them some money if I had any.

Past the Theatre Royal,
past the Forum,
cut through the market,
seagulls circling.
I see a mural that reads:

NORWICH: A CITY OF STORIES

I'm learning already,
from what Lucas said
in one of the workshops the other day,
that everyone here seems to be
some kind of writer
of novels, poems or plays.

I walk past The Book Hive and look at
all the different covers on display.
Before, I would have just walked past
but I think I'm starting to
appreciate books more now –
not just the image on the front either
but the words inside too.

Until the other week, basically, I thought
creative writing was kind of dry
but both Mr Bruce and the sessions with Lucas
are starting to make me notice new things
about literature I never noticed before.

Some of the books look proper interesting
and I recognize some of the names of the authors
from TV or online somewhere.

I don't feel like going in though;
can't put my finger on it but sometimes bookshops
can feel a little intimidating to me,
like people might think
I'm not smart enough
to deserve the luxury
of going inside or something.
Or like I'm some kind of thief
who doesn't intend to pay.

So I walk away, past the busker
singing some half-recognizable song –
Dermot Kennedy or George Ezra maybe –

have a quick look at the Rolexes on display
and dream about wearing one one day.

I see a poster for Wild Paths festival
and even though I don't recognize
any of the artists playing,
I still think it's cool that there's live music
at all these venues to go and see
in the flesh, if you wanted to.

March past Jarrolds, L'Hexagone and Turtle Bay.

After walking around a bit,
taking it all in, I decide
that I probably have all the material I need
to answer Mr Bruce's question, and
I'm starting to feel
a little bit tired and hungry,
which isn't ideal
when you don't have much money.

The buses here are actually a bit expensive
compared to London and I haven't
got a proper pass yet, so I start to make
the long walk home back through the city
past the peng-looking pastries
in Bread Source on Upper St Giles Street,
just as it starts to rain pretty heavily and
a special blue bus full of posh-looking
private school students
whizzes by and splashes me,
drenching me from afro to toe.

In class the next day,
I use my notes
from my walk to respond
to the prompt Mr Bruce set.

As I turn my observations
into more of a structured mini-story
with proper paragraphs
and more complete sentences,
I sprinkle in some sibilance
for extra descriptive spice,
add some listing,
and chuck in a compound adjective or two.

And just before the end of the day,
I drop what I've written on Sir's desk
in the corner of the classroom:
two and a half sides of A4.
Pretty sure that's more
than I've ever written
in English before.

The following Monday,
at the beginning of the lesson
Sir says in a semi-smug way
that we're all very lucky
to have such a hard-working
and diligent English teacher,
who doesn't have much of a

life on the weekends, apparently
(his words, not mine),
because he has already
marked our descriptive writing pieces
that we handed in just last week.

He starts handing the sheets of paper back
to Riley, to Eva, to Dylan, to Evie, to Leigh
and smiles broadly when he gets to me.
I can't quite believe it: Grade 9, full marks,
forty out of forty.

NOVEMBER

**Ever since my top mark in English
Mr Bruce has been
making a proper fuss of me,
using my work as a model
on the interactive whiteboard
to show other students what they can do
to get top marks too.**

He's been underlining lines that stand out,
unpacking the wider connotations
of some of my references,
coming up with these far-fetched explanations
of what the writer (me) was intending by
writing such-and-such a phrase.

To be honest, I just wrote it.

But for the last few lessons,
usually as the starter activity,
Sir's used a quote
of one of the paragraphs I wrote
from that now-famous
descriptive writing piece
inspired by my random walk around the city,
and gets the class to
comment on what I did well.

It was kinda blessed at first,
all that attention made me feel good inside,
but it's also getting
a bit embarrassing now too.

At breaktime, chilling in our usual spot
in the corner of the quadrant,
Leigh continues to take the piss out of me.
'So when you gonna write your next
masterpiece then, Shakespeare?'
he jokes, as he gestures extravagantly,
pretending to write something
with a fancy feather quill while pulling
a sort of snobbish *la-di-da* face at me.

It's only because me and Leigh
have actually become
quite good friends recently
that I let him take the piss a bit.
I like how's he's just pretty carefree
and not afraid to be himself basically.
Now he's wearing
bright pinkish nail varnish
even though I'm sure it's
against school rules.

To my relief, to spare my blushes,
the conversation soon turns
to the upcoming football trials
this weekend, the ones
for the Norwich City academy
that're taking place this Saturday at UEA,
the pitches owned by the local university.

Leigh, who used to play a bit
before he got bored, apparently,

and claims he used to be a baller, says
he might come along but admits that he prefers
watching boys playing it than
the match itself these days.

I used to play for Impact Football Academy
back in Hackney, and played for the school team
alongside Maz in central midfield.
We had the best partnership
in the middle of the park.
I think our friendship off the pitch
helped our performance on it.
We were a dynamic duo that
made all the other schools scared.

So I back myself to know that if I
show up on Saturday,
I'm sure I have a good chance
of catching a scout's eye.

I like playing centre-mid,
breaking down the play,
having the vision to execute the right ball
at the right time to the attacking players.
I'm just in the process of telling all this to Leigh
when all of a sudden I see Malachi,
this Year Eleven boy, approach us
out the corner of my eye.

It's not raining and it's not even that cold
but he has the hood of his Canada Goose up,

which gets my back up straightaway.
When you've lived where I have,
seen what I've seen,
you've gotta have eyes in the
back of your head basically,
in case anyone tries a madness,
which can be tiring,
necessary but so tiring.

I've seen him about, Malachi,
roaming around the school,
while teachers trot behind him trying to keep up,
negotiating plea bargains
to get him back into class.

'You good?' he asks.
Looking me dead in the eyes.

'Yeah, yeah,' I say, spudding him back.

He deliberately ignores Leigh completely,
who's pulling quite funny
overdramatic faces behind Malachi's back
in response to being spurned.

Leigh told me the other day
that they went to the same primary.
Apparently, he was actually all right back then –
quite quiet and kept himself to himself.
But by the end of Year Seven,
beginning of Year Eight maybe,

just started hanging around with the wrong crowd,
started mixing with olders with bad reputations
and selling things I bet he was too young
to really understand the consequences of.

'Listen, London boy,' he mumbles,
speaking through gritted teeth mainly,
'if you ever wanna chat business some time,
get in touch, innit. Can get you
little jobs here and there,'
he says, looking over his shoulder suspiciously
as if under surveillance by the feds
or being watched by rival opps,
but there's no one else anywhere near,
just some fresh Year Seven in his oversized blazer,
struggling to tie his shoelace.

'I got you, innit,' he adds,
as he spuds me again and bops away.

It's an interaction I find pretty funny
in all honesty, because as hard as Malachi
thinks he is, because he
might know a few Norfolk boys
who might sell things they shouldn't
now and again,
that's nothing compared to
what London life is like
and some of the stuff I've seen
on the **wild streets of east**.
Like teenagers, boys like Maz,
stabbed to death for no reason at all.

So I take this interaction with a pinch of salt.
I haven't travelled all those miles from London,
changed schools, moved away
from friends and family,
started my whole life again basically,
to get involved in some
amateur county lines nonsense
just because I'm a Black boy from Hackney.
I didn't come all the way here
to get myself messed up with wannabe
roadmen. **Not again.**

ᵐⁱⁱ|ⁱⁱ|ⁱⁱⁱ

It's Friday, which means instead of English
we have another poetry session in the
drama studio with Lucas.

Today's Five-minute Free-write starts with the line:
'Play the bloody song!' the girl shouted at the DJ.

The five minutes have already begun,
so I start scribbling and, as instructed to,
write the first thing that comes in my head.
I'm getting better, I think, about not caring
and just letting my thoughts run wild.

Leigh, who always sits next to me
these days, in both English and in these Friday
sessions with Lucas,
is getting the hang of it too and starts

writing with ease, line after line, all the way from
the left margin to the right.

Unlike some of the others in the class,
I'm not yet ready to share what I end up writing,
even though Lucas tries to coax me
into just reading a line or two
from the paragraphs I've scribbled.
Maybe next week, I always say,
which seems to work
and so far is thankfully buying me more time.

The next activity is even more strange.
Lucas tells us to write as the title on a fresh page:
9 Possible Reasons for Throwing a Cat into a Wheelie Bin
He gives us the first line to begin.

1) You mistook the cat for a crisp packet
2) _____
3) _____
4) _____
5) _____
6) _____
7) _____
8) _____
9) _____

'This is an activity inspired by the poem
a fantastic poet called Caroline Bird
wrote in response to a news story
about a woman from Coventry,' Lucas tells us.

'Who for some random reason, as she was
walking past this cat, stroked it
and then just dropped the unsuspecting feline
in a wheelie bin and walked off.'

Unluckily for her it was caught on CCTV,
which Lucas shows us footage of on the whiteboard
by playing this *Sky News* clip on YouTube, and
asks us to write another eight reasons
why someone might drop a cat into a wheelie.

'The more creative the better,'
he exclaims energetically,
'like *the cat demanded to be lifted in telepathically*;
anything at all – go crazy,
and your five minutes start . . .'
– he looks down at his silver Casio watch – 'now.'

I throw myself right in,
into the **deep end**,
teaching myself to swim.

I actually enjoyed this activity, and, at last,
after a few weeks of being super sceptical,
I think I'm starting to like being creative and
messing around with poetry.
Unlike how I thought before,
it doesn't have to take itself too seriously.
There is room to be a bit silly with it sometimes.

After a long week,
you just can't beat that feeling
of basking in the freedom of a Saturday
when's there's no school,
no wrist-squeezing chains.
It's Saturday, '*Carpe diem*,'
I've heard people say,
meaning, I think,
time to seize the day.

And today is a big day –
it's the Norwich City
football trial at UEA.

I got a bit overexcited before I went to sleep,
so I've got everything more or less packed already –
kit and boots; I'm feeling nervous but ready.

To prepare, I've been watching
as many games as I can –
full-length highlights on YouTube
of all the top European leagues:
France, Italy, Spain and Germany,
and of course *Match of the Day*.

I've been playing FIFA,
reading articles on BBC Sport,
following all the transfer news
on social media, and,
when there's a United game on normal telly,
screaming the house down when we score.

I'm not saying today will be a walk in the park,
but I have enough in the locker
to impress anyone who's watching.

With a spring in my step, I sprint downstairs
and into the kitchen,
hoping there's some fruit juice left,
but when I open the fridge,
it's pretty empty –
much of the shopping bought on Wednesday
has gone already.

There's a drop of Robinsons left
and a couple of custard creams in the cupboard
that will have to do for now,
cos Mum is always telling me
it's never good to leave the house on an
empty stomach, even though
there's never *that* much food in the house
to begin with.

As I scoff the biscuits and
wash them down with a very weak squash,
I can hear Mum upstairs rummaging and rifling
through her drawers, which is a
little strange because she doesn't usually
start work till much later on a Saturday.

She's had a lot on her plate recently –
the stress of the move and how hard she's
had to work to help the transition

from London to this new city go smoothly,
and how it's all been taking its toll
on her mood and health for the last few weeks;
longer than that actually.

'Mum,' I shout from the
bottom of the stairs,
'I can hear you getting ready.
Where you going?'

She comes out of her room and
takes a few steps down
to be heard more clearly.
'With you, silly boy, of course;
coming to watch you play
before I start my shift,' she says.

I'm dead.

I don't even remember
telling her about it.
And the idea of going to these
potentially life-changing
football trials with my mum
fills me with dread.

'Mum, **no**, you'll just get cold,
trust me,' I say,
but before I can put
her off any more she's gone
back upstairs already,
to finish getting ready.

The pitches are a ten-minute walk away,
and as we make our way there
I'm just trying to focus on how I intend to play;
trying to picture pinging
defence-splitting balls
and making darting runs
through the middle and,
if in the right position to at any time,
slotting the ball home calmly
past the helpless keeper
and celebrating with my team-mates.

We arrive just as the tracksuited coaches,
with their clipboards,
divide the large group of
players into two teams,
flinging fluorescent bibs at them:
orange versus green.

But all of a sudden,
standing at a distance to them,
something doesn't quite feel right;
all of a sudden I'm feeling too shy.

Every time I try a little step forward,
I take a bigger one back.
And now Mum is physically pushing me to go.
But every bit of my body is just saying **'no'**.

In my hearts of hearts
I know I'm good enough to play.
I have the vision, first touch and tenacity . . .
but my confidence's gone.
Shot to bits. Devoid of all energy.

I look up to the sky and think of Maz.

'What's the matter, Ronny?' Mum asks.
'This isn't like you; it's about to kick off,
you better hurry up,' she adds.

She can read the worry written on my face.
I don't really know what to say,
not sure how to answer,
I just feel kinda frozen and
it's not just cos it's cold.
It's something else.
Something deeper inside,
some unfelt anxiety
stopping me from doing
what I love doing usually.

I guess without Maz by my side,
it's not so easy to take big moments
like this in my stride.

I can now see, from here,
on the outskirts of the playing fields,
that the match is about to begin and the players
shuffle into their starting positions,

desperate to get a few early
touches on the ball,
settle any early nerves they might have.

But I'm just standing here
in my kit, with my woolly hat and gloves,
looking on at the others showing off their skills
and having fun, and I feel stupid for
feeling so insecure but I can't bring myself
to join in. Invisible hands hold me back,
deny me permission.

And as I watch on from afar,
I feel my eyes suddenly
go all heavy, all stingy and
sore, and then I sense
something unstoppable surging through me . . .
One tear, then two, slide down my
face and drip down my chin.
I wipe them away with a gloved hand
as Mum puts her arm round my shoulder
and leads the way back home saying,
'It's OK, sweetheart, it's OK.'

It's the end of double English and
I am in the middle of packing my stuff away
and heading to break when Mr Bruce says,
'Ronny, before you go, can I have a quick word?'

My heart beats hard and fast for a moment,
because I don't think I've done anything wrong?

After a weird start getting used to everything:

– **new city**
– **new school**
– **new systems**

and, of course, trying to cope with
what happened to Maz and stuff,
I've just been keeping my head
down to stay out of trouble,
trying to apply myself in my lessons, especially
in English, a subject I kinda
rate now and actually
think I'm making good progress with this year.

'I heard you didn't do the football trial,' Sir says,
his eyes focused on mine intensely.
'Which is a real shame, Ronny, because
Mr Martin's told me – many times, actually –
just how good he thinks you are already.'

I've been trying to forget
about the trial for the last few days.
I still can't really explain
what went wrong on Saturday,
why my body was willing me not to play.
I was trying to figure it out
while moping about the house all of Sunday.

'Look, these things happen,' Mr Bruce says,
'and I'm sure you'll get another chance,
in fact, I have a glorious opportunity for you.'

I didn't know Sir was a football fan
but perhaps he's got something up his sleeve:
another trial with another team lined up for me.
Norwich's bitter rivals, Ipswich Town, maybe,
or he's mates with the manager of
semi-professional Mulbarton, possibly.

'There's a very special
and exclusive trip,' he starts,
'to a writing retreat
during the February half-term.
It's up in Shropshire, not too far from Wales,
and is a fantastic chance for you
to write even more spectacular stories,
or even your own collection of poetry.'

A **big**, **big blow**,
not quite the football news
I'd hoped for.

'You know already
how much your descriptive
writing piece impressed me,
and Lucas is pleased with how you've
been doing with him on Fridays –'

'Sir,' I feel the need to interrupt before
he says any more.
'I'm honoured to be asked,
I really am – thank you –
but I don't think this is something for me.
I like writing songs but don't consider
myself a creative writer of poetry.'

But he's not taking 'no' for an answer.

'Ronny, just so you know,
as it stands, only one person
from the whole school gets to go.
I think this is a wonderful opportunity
to learn and improve and I've already
spoken to the Head of English,
and I want that place to go to you.

'You don't have to decide right away;
have a little think, chat to Mum,
and let me know by . . .
the end of next week, let's say.'

'Will do, Sir, will do; I better go,'
I say, mindlessly combing out my Afro,
not really able to take it all in,
focusing instead on untangling the kinks.

DECEMBER

**I've been noticing recently
that, like me, Leigh
is letting his hair grow out.**

But whereas my Afro is getting
taller, bigger and wider,
his is getter longer and straighter
like that singer Sam Ryder.

Even though some teachers
when they see me down the corridors,
in the hall, quad, or out in the playground,
look at my ever-growing Afro kinda strangely,
they never actually say anything
and I know it's only because
no one else in the whole school
(maybe even the whole city?)
has hair like me,
that they're probably just intrigued.

I doubt it's because they have
some kind of issue with me,
or take offence at the
way I look personally.

Leigh's grown his nails longer too,
and recently he's been painting them a
really bright blue,
which I can't lie I found a bit weird
and something you definitely
wouldn't get away

with at school back in Hackney.
But people here generally seem to be
more accepting and it would actually
be kind of strange of me
to act a certain way towards him,
just because he likes to do his own thing.
To be honest, I really
respect it, if anything.

Today we've got a mock exam,
the first one of many this week –
English Literature now,
English Language after break.

'Bubble tea later?' asks Leigh,
as we shuffle into the hall half-heartedly.
I'm not overly keen
cos it always annoys me
when the big bits of whatever it is
get stuck in the straw, but as we
were planning to go into town anyway,
to pass through the new funfair in Chapelfields,
I think *Why not* and say,
'Yeah, all right then, sure.'

'Grand, good luck, Shakespeare,' he says,
as we shuffle in and try to find the right desk
with our candidate number on,
while teachers bark out instructions,
directing the swarm of sad-looking students
to their correct seats.

I'm feeling all right about it if I'm honest,
even though I haven't really
revised all that much.
Out of all the subjects, I feel like
English is the one I can blag the best
and, with the help of Mr Bruce this year,
I think I'm getting better at it too,
definitely enjoying it more than I used to.

With everyone now in the right place
the hall goes quiet as Mr Flotman,
the Head of English, gives his
final instructions and students
start scribbling down their name,
candidate number (again)
and who their English teacher is
at the top of the page.

The exam begins
and I'm just about to start writing
my response to the essay question:
'HOW DOES PRIESTLEY EXPLORE
GUILT IN *AN INSPECTOR CALLS*?'
when all of a sudden Malachi bursts in
through the double doors
and starts bopping about and shouting,
'We outside, bro! We outside!'

He probably wouldn't sit them anyway but
his year are not even doing exams this week.
So the teachers are on edge immediately and

despite many of them trying to stop Malachi,
he continues doing his own thing, circling
the whole of the hall proper hyperactively,
and even threats that they'll
send for Mr Shaughnessy
don't seem to frighten him.

You can tell his head's gone,
that he's not in the right space to listen.
Not really taking in what anyone says,
as he just continues bopping about
in between and around the desks,
occasionally rubbing people's heads
with his trademark gloved hand,
like that Curley character from *Of Mice and Men*.
The one who likes to start trouble for no reason.

There's always some kind of story
being whispered about Malachi,
about why he might act the way he
does in school.

Everyone knows what he's like now,
so just ignore him,
have been conditioned to not give him
the attention when he's
in one of these mad moods.

Thankfully he hasn't noticed me and
soon a pack of teachers manage to corner him,
calm him down enough to get him to sit

at the back of the hall and just chill,
far enough away to be out of sight to many
and get the exam going again.

After the distraction
of Malachi's interruption,
I'm ready to start writing again
when suddenly there's some
commotion at the front
that ripples further and further back,
till it becomes a **full-blown eruption of noise**,
a chorus of high-pitched,
ear-splitting screams.

Students leap from their seats,
shocked, alarmed, excited.
Silly, scared, shrilly screams
are amplified like a speaker
on the highest volume
echoing all around the hall.

From here, near the back, it's unclear
if it's a bomb or an armed intruder.
For once, it's nothing to do with Malachi,
because he's still sitting against the back wall
being talked and tended to by teachers.

Then as the students begin to creep, leap
and run from the front, suddenly I see
the cause of this out-of-control scene.

Two small eyes.
Ears pinned all the way back.
Nose sniffing about frantically.

Somehow, from somewhere,
literally appearing out of nowhere,
a small deer has got into the exam hall.

It's clearly completely terrified and is
making this really loud screeching bark
as it tries to find its way back out
to the safety of somewhere familiar,
back out into the wild,
or somewhere like Steeple Tower Park.

I'm just standing over my desk,
not really scared but stunned,
as Leigh comes and joins me.
'Nah, this is mad,' I say.
'You don't get deer in Hackney.'

'That's a muntjac, you dummy.'

'A what?'

'A muntjac. You see *a lot* of dead ones
on the roads round here,
their guts splattered all over the tarmac;
all that blood and stuff, it's really disgusting
and also quite sad,' Leigh says,
as we edge closer and closer to the back.

Despite clearly being scared, lost and terrified,
the little muntjac suddenly
makes a desperate beeline towards Malachi,
who, unlike the rest of the hall,
is strangely calmer now
than he was five minutes ago.

Squatting down, Malachi gestures
for it to come over and
the little deer pauses in its tracks,
looks at Malachi then looks back.

It stops whining as it creeps closer and,
as Malachi cups his hands,
the little muntjac,
that just a few seconds before was running wild,
is now sniffing Malachi's hands and fingers,
feeling all calm, all safe, all loved.

·ıı||ıı||ıııı

It's a cold and dark December Wednesday,
the last week before the Christmas holiday,
and even though there's a big
fairylight-lit tree in the hall,
tinsel that's been Blu-Tacked
around corridor displays,
and a big Christmas lunch planned for Friday,
as I sit at the very back of
Mr Bruce's English classroom,
I'm not feeling particularly festive.

I've never enjoyed Christmas
like that, to be honest,
it's not a big thing in our family.
I've never had enough personally to
buy anything for Mum, and she's never really
been blessed with that kind of P
to spend on me.

I haven't eaten Christmas cake
or watched the Queen's Speech on TV,
never had an advent calendar or put up a tree,
never been too keen on eating really dry turkey
(still not that nice even when drenched in gravy),
and because of my ever-growing Afro,
them tissue-paper Christmas hats don't fit me.

Right now, there's some kind
of festive light tunnel
in the city everyone is
taking pictures under
to post on their Insta stories,
but I can't be bothered to go,
or watch the panto.

I quite like the fact there's a few weeks
off school, obviously,
time to chill a bit and watch *Elf* and *Home Alone*
(one and two), but that's it really.
When it comes down to it,
Christmas is just another day for me.

Even though Mr Bruce is giving up his free time
to lead this after-school revision session,
I just feel too tired, too unmotivated
to do any more work today.
So instead of working on the essay
question that Mr Bruce has set us,
I'm at the back messing around with Leigh.

'No expense spared!' Sir says
because he's splashed out and
bought packets of Rich Tea
but, despite pocketing a little handful,
I still can't concentrate so I go to the toilet
to clear my head and stretch my legs.

In films and stuff,
I've seen the main character splash water
on their face to wake themselves up.
But it's too cold for that
and then afterwards my skin would get all dry
and some of my hair might even get wet,
making the front of it all frizzy.
So instead I slap my cheeks a bit,
applying enough pressure to hopefully
snap myself out of this tired state I'm in.

But as I gargle some water,
all of a sudden I hear something
coming from one of the cubicles.

It's hard to work out what it is exactly,
but it seems someone is
panting and wheezing heavily
to such an extent,
they're struggling to breathe.
Then I hear something falling to the ground,
something plastic perhaps,
followed by a much larger thump
like a body slumped,
followed by a sort of crash,
like someone's head slamming into the toilet seat
with an ungraceful **thud**.

There's definitely someone in there,
and whoever's inside doesn't sound like
they're in a good way.

You all right in there?
I shout to no answer, leaving the sink
to get a little closer to investigate.

So after thinking about it for less than a second,
I decide to act on instinct and take action.
By giving it a little nudge, it's clear
the cubicle door is not only locked
but judging by the bit
of shoe sticking out the bottom,
also blocked by whoever is inside.
So I go into the one next door, which is free,
to see what I can do to help

whoever it is who's in distress,
and got themselves into this mess.

As I peep over the top I can't believe what I see.
I'm so stunned and shocked,
I'm also proper struggling to breathe.
Lying there, half sprawled across the toilet seat
and half on the floor, yellow rubber gloves on
with the plastic brush falling out of her grasp is
not someone I expected to be here.

I can't see her face but
it's obvious straightaway,
and she's there all crooked and bent.
Showing no signs of life,
no flicker, flinch or twitch,
she looks . . . out of it.
I have no idea what she's doing here,
wearing a cleaner's uniform in my school,
branded apron and Marigolds.

But that doesn't matter right now
because, right in front of my eyes,
below me, squashed
against the wall of the cubicle,
my poor mum looks all lifeless and dead.

I'm completely frozen,
heart beating too fast,
thoughts too slow and I'm still
struggling struggling to catch my breath.

Struggling to find the word at first
but then it comes: **'Mum!'** I shout.
'Mum!' I shout again.

I need to get help urgently.

I run out of the bathroom,
sprint down the corridor and
burst into Mr Bruce's classroom,
to tell him what's happened.

Mr Bruce, who's in the middle of
going through Question 1 answers,
reassures me everything is going to be OK,
then immediately gets caretaker Barry's help.

Barry, who's usually moody
and doesn't regularly
make the effort to say hello, manages to
force the door open, push Mum's legs
to one side and nudge it
just enough to squeeze through
and pull Mum out of the cubicle.

Yes, there's a big gash on her head;
yes, she's exhausted and her blood sugar's low
and her ECG numbers were worryingly off the chart
according to the paramedics, but she's alive,
came around five minutes or so after me finding her,
and was adamant that she was
well enough to not need to go to hospital.

For years I've seen her
come home late from work, with
swollen bags under her eyes,
her black cheeks red from the cold,
having taken three buses across London instead
of the Tube, which is more expensive.

For years Mum's been working three jobs
to keep me clothed and fed
and warm at night in my own blow-up bed,
and provided the right springboard
for me to find my feet and flourish in this world.

And I know it hasn't been
easy doing it on her own.
Being a single mum to a newborn isn't fun,
especially when there's a ton of bills to pay.

Having a child these days
is expensive, in a society
divided by the **haves** and **have-nots**.

It's tough staying on top
of the ever-shifting trends
and things are getting more expensive:
clothes, kreps, food –
it seems it costs a fortune just to breathe.

In my bedroom back in London,
there was this thick black mould
growing on one of the walls,

right there next to where I lay my head,
that, over the years living there,
got deep into my lungs and spread
multiplied and mutated and
it felt like it was **swallowing me up whole . . .**

But the council didn't want to know.

It's stuff like that
that gets lodged in your brain,
keeps you up in the middle of the night,
dreaming of living a better life
without roads in the ends
being cordoned off constantly;
without needing to add water to your
shop-brand cornflakes for breakfast;
unhealthily wet walls,
dingy curtains and dirty carpets
and being too scared to open
the door when it's knocked
in case it's a bailiff, burglar
or a jealous ex-partner of Mum's.

Down the years I've seen new boyfriends
(so, so many, in all honesty)
come and go, some much better than others.
I know she's found it hard to find
love at times.
Maybe some men didn't fancy
going out with someone
with a young boy
to look after too.

Kemi was a good one,
stayed longer than the rest and
treated us both right,
showed us love and was generally nice –
the way my dad should have been really.

I was gutted when they broke up.
Things didn't go to plan and *the relationship
just sort of ran its course* is what Mum said.

So after all she's been through I
just want to make my mum **proud**,
doing something I **enjoy**,
rapping to earn enough **money**
to **look after** both her and me,
and that's why I'm **determined**
to do all I can do to make her **happy**.

Because right now,
here in the safety of Mr Bruce's classroom,
Mum looks all shaken and exhausted,
quietly sipping from a plastic cup of water and
being hugged by a worried colleague.
And as I go to give her a hug too,
she whispers, *Sorry*
in my ear, like she's done something wrong.

Turns out Mum's been
working here for a few weeks now;
asked her colleague
from the primary school she works at
for a few extra shifts to try

and earn some extra money
to get us through Christmas.

Mr Bruce orders Five Guys on Deliveroo
even though Mum tells him not to,
assures him not to make a fuss,
telling him she's already defrosted the mince.
But he insists, and thirty minutes later he's
clutching brown paper bags
full of bacon cheeseburgers, with
lettuce and ketchup and chips, for everyone.

Leigh, who's been by my side
the whole evening,
gives me a warm smile as
I bite into my burger and Mum
timidly nibbles on a chip,
looking all sad and defeated
but also grateful for the
generosity of Mr Bruce.

And after what's happened this evening
I'm even more determined
to work hard for our future, including
revising over the holidays so I'm in
a decent position for the mocks when we
come back in the new term.

JANUARY

I'm still weighing up
the pros and cons
of going on this writing
residential in a few weeks.

I know it's a chance to see
a new part of the country,
to get away from Norwich for a bit,
have a little change of scenery,
but I was really debating whether to leave
especially after what happened to Mum.
But she assured me not to worry
and told me to give it a go.

Though I don't think I'm a poet,
I do like writing lines that rhyme sometimes.
And I can't lie, I'm starting to loosen
up a bit and enjoy these Friday sessions more.
I've flicked through my notebook and,
just in these sessions with Lucas alone,
I've written twenty new pieces already. **Twenty.**

The quality of them is mixed;
not all of them bang, some are
better than others obviously,
but that's a pretty mad achievement really,
considering I didn't much rate poetry
before, or think of myself as
someone with the talent
to write some of the lines I have written,
in all honesty.

And now, I actually kinda
look forward to these sessions,
see them as a chance to express myself
in a different kind of way.
An opportunity to **experiment**, to **create**
that doesn't necessarily have to make
complete sense,
can be a **little strange,**
doesn't have to have
clever puns or a **catchy hook.**
It can just be whatever you're
feeling at the time.
It doesn't even have to rhyme.

'Proud of yourself, aren't ya, Shakespeare?'
Leigh says as he pulls out his chair next to me
at the table in the corner at the back, as always,
and plonks himself down theatrically,
having spotted me looking back on
some of the pieces I wrote previously.

I close my notebook sheepishly,
annoyed that he's a bit right and, secondly,
that he keeps using this
embarrassing new nickname for me.

'Call me that one more time and I swear . . .'
I threaten, with my backhand raised
but with a broad smile on my face.

'I'm pooped,' he says,
as he puffs out his cheeks,
making the edges of his
ever-growing fringe quiver.
'Need a moment
to catch my breath properly.
Mr Martin works us mad hard in PE
these days,' he says,
as he delves into his Hoodrich bag to retrieve
his VOSS water bottle,
with a piece of sliced lemon in it,
and downs it all in one.

'Ah yeah, that's the
good shit!' Leigh says,
clearly delighted to be
finally rehydrated.

Instead of doing our usual
Five-minute Free-write
to start the session, Lucas goes round the
tables of two and hands out individually
wrapped fortune cookies.

He instructs us to open them up
and read the note inside.
'Have a look, consider the deeper meaning
of the message and use the words
to write an extended piece.'

You can hear the cracks from the
rest of the class, just seconds apart,
as they break their cookie
in two and seek to
discover their truth.

Leigh's laughing his head off
within seconds of opening his.
THE QUIETER YOU ARE
THE MORE YOU HEAR
it says, and when he looks at the little paper again,
starts laughing hysterically, proper loudly.

I leave him to compose himself
and open mine,
which is kinda blessed, I think.
YOU HAVE TO BE IN IT TO WIN IT
Nothing mind-blowing, it's a phrase I've heard before
and is pretty easy to understand,
but is still kind of inspirational.

I write down the fortune
as the title at the top of my page and
jot down the first few words
that come into my head as I nibble on my cookie,
which is proper crunchy but still tasty.

I write and bite. Bite and write.

Another session,
another new task that's a bit wacky.

I have to admire Lucas for his originality.
He's always coming up with these
mad new activities,
always thinking outside the box
to keep us on our toes,
to try and keep us engaged.
Fair play.
I never know
what he's got in store for us every Friday.

This piece I'm writing, I can tell,
is turning into more of a song.
There's lots of little bits of rhyme in there
and the beginning of a chorus maybe,
but I'm not tryna force it –
it's all coming out pretty naturally.

Anytime I get a little stuck, **hit a rock**,
suffer from temporary **writer's block**,
I look back at the fortune again –
YOU HAVE TO BE IN IT TO WIN IT –
and a new line comes back into my head.
Something about **football**,
something about **songwriting**,
something about **school**,
something about **Maz**.

A whirlwind of emotions,
this weird combination of
pure joy and **gut-wrenching distress**;
idea after **idea**,

image after **image**,
line after **line**,
and before I know it,
time is up.

I've nearly got a whole page,
written so much
my wrist hurts.

'So . . .' Lucas begins, as always,
'there's no pressure to share
but I would love to hear
how you engaged with
your little prophecy.'

I think about it for a second and
for the first time I put my
hand up halfway
and say, 'Yeah, go on then,
I'll share a bit of mine.'
Everyone looks towards me,
at the back in the corner.
'Well, I thought I'd never see the day,'
Lucas says, clutching his beanie to his chest
like it's a flat cap, and
putting on a croaky-old-man accent.

I read the first couple of
words but Lucas suddenly
interrupts me and asks,
'Could you do me a favour, please, Ronny?'

Could you very possibly stand up for me?
It's better for the delivery.'

I pull a face, like he's asking a bit much,
but I start to stand up reluctantly,
when suddenly the drama studio door
swings open with a **bang**, making
everyone look away from me
and towards the noise immediately.

In marches Malachi on some madness,
charging about on another mission to cause chaos.
No blazer, shirt untucked, tie all loose,
baggy trousers and black Air Forces on.
I sit down again real quick before he clocks
that I was just about to pour out my heart
and read my piece to the rest of the class.

He's on one, you can tell;
his face is all twisted,
he looks kinda vex and excited,
his eyes are all glazed and mischievous and
his clothes smell a bit like weed.
He's acting like one of those
XL bully dogs in the park
let loose by the owner from its lead.

I can hear music being played off his phone.
It's a song I know –
'London Scammer' by Tankz.
I can hear it even though

the sound is all muffled coming from the pocket
of the tracksuit bottoms that he's wearing
underneath his sagging school trousers.

Lucas doesn't really know what to do
or how to react, just sort of stands back,
and there's no other (proper) teacher in sight.
I see no one through the open door,
nobody at all walking down the corridor.
Meanwhile, Malachi's bopping from table to table,
snatching pieces of paper, scanning
them disinterestedly, then dashing them on the floor
and pulling faces at the creative pieces
some of the others have been writing
in their notebooks like he's appalled
by our attempts to express ourselves with words.
Or even worse, poetry.

'What's this?' he asks, as he picks up
someone's unopened fortune cookie and
asks Lucas, **'Oi, let me get one?'**

'Erm, yeah . . . I think I've . . .
I've got a spare cookie you can have.'
Lucas looks over his shoulder at the whole
big box of them nervously.
For the first time he's not being
the boisterous and carefree
ball of energy we're used to seeing;
around Malachi he's all nervous and panicky.

Lucas whispers something to Evie
sitting in the very front row, one of the really
good girls in my year, and then shortly
after she scuttles out the class to probably
find another teacher or the head teacher,
Mr Shaughnessy, to come get Malachi.

Malachi charges about a bit more
and then spots me sat in the corner
next to Leigh, and makes a beeline.
'Yes, yes, London boy!' he says,
then gives me a spud.
I notice, yet again, he's wearing just the one glove;
even Leigh doesn't seem to know
whether it's a fashion statement
or if there's something about
his hand he wants to hide.

He crooks his head and stares suspiciously
at my notebook,
which is firmly closed in front of me
with both my elbows pressed down
hard on top.

He's probably wondering
what I've been writing but chooses
not to ask in the end, which is a relief.
'Know someone who wants to meet you, bro,'
he says. 'A business opportunity,
a chance to make an extra bit of money,'
he whispers loudly.

I play along, pretend to be interested;
concentrate on what he's saying, nod my head
at the right times, even though I know
I don't want to get mixed up in any of the business
he's talking about. I bet it's not the kind
of deals you might see on that programme
The Apprentice or whatever it's called.

'Furthermore, drop your digits in this,' he says
as he hands me his brand-new iPhone
with the music still playing.
Now it's Nutcase22's whistle song 'Swing'.
I don't really wanna give him my number,
and I can feel the heat of Leigh's eyes on me,
but it feels like I have no other
choice in this situation,
like there's this weird pressure pressing
down on my shoulders.
So I reluctantly thumb in my number
and hand him back his phone.

'I'll drop you a message soon, yeah?' he says
and, just as I'm about to reply,
in comes Evie with Mrs Barnham-Broom,
the deputy. With a face that's
all **tight** and **taut**,
thunderous and **fierce**,
she glares at Malachi,
who doesn't put up much
of a fight. Instead says, 'Cool,'
just as he always does,

and slowly starts walking towards the door that
just two or three minutes earlier he
had barged in through.
'Later, dickheads!' he says out loud
for everyone to hear.
'Enjoy your stupid cookie poetry.'

It takes a minute or two for the whole class to
settle down again, cos there's a volatility
to Malachi that makes any room he's
in **sharp** and **spiky**,
that shifts the energy completely.

'So . . .' Lucas begins, clearly still a little rattled
by the interruption, 'where were we?'

He definitely remembers
that I was about to read
a bit of my piece,
but that was before,
and now I don't feel like reading it any more,
so I put my head down and try to avoid his gaze.
Lucas knows not to push it and instead
starts explaining what activity
we're going to do next.

I don't know how he
managed to grab two, but
Leigh's got another fortune cookie
and now he's
ripping the wrapper open and
cracking it apart.

He reads the words carefully,
pauses, takes in every bit
and shows me without saying anything.
YOU WILL TRAVEL TO
MANY PLACES IN THE WORLD.
Leigh looks at the little slip
of paper again, amazed,
then towards me, as if the words are
some kinda special revelation,
some divine DM from above.

'It's a sign, Ronny, it has to be,' he whispers.
'During break we have to find Mr Bruce.
You know that writing trip he told you about?
I *have* to come with you.
This –' he says, waving the little slip
in front of my face
like it's a winning lottery ticket for millions –
'is a message from the goddesses.'
He says it looking up towards
the ceiling of the drama studio.

I'm sure the fortune cookie is probably
referring to somewhere
like Dubai or the South of France,
Cancun or the Caribbean and not
some random place in Shropshire, but to be fair
I quite like the idea of Leigh coming with me
to keep me company
throughout the week,

so I'm happy to play along and
find Mr Bruce at breaktime.

᠁᠁᠁᠁

'Guess who's definitely coming
to Shropshire with ya!' Leigh says,
shimmying his hips and whining his waist
like he's a contestant on *Strictly*,
or he's expecting the week to be
as exciting as some completely
parent-free underage party.

Thankfully for Leigh
(and me, in all honesty),
someone from another school
has dropped out and there was
another place free.

So now it's settled,
we're both going to
some random house
in the middle of nowhere
during the February half-term
to write poems . . . and stuff.

We were told people spend
hundreds of pounds for a week
at Arvon, so this place
must be pretty special,

and I'm trying really hard
to look forward to it,
to make the most of it,
see it as an opportunity to
do something creative that might
also help Mum out in future maybe.

It hasn't sunk in yet really, but
Mr Bruce has assured me
that the school can help provide
any bits that I might need
when I'm there.

I like Mr Bruce, he's
quite chill about most things usually,
but it's five minutes until
the end of the school day and
he's moaning to us again about glue sticks.
Saying he gave out fifteen
at the start of the lesson
and has only got fourteen back.

Complaining about
the measly English budget
and how money spent
rebuying lost glue sticks
means less money for trips.

It's only because Mr Bruce is
one of the safe teachers
that, unlike the rest of the class,

I show some genuine
desire to find it.

We all sort of half look around us,
under tables and behind chairs,
no one caring that much, really,
knowing that it'll probably
turn up at some point,
and all of us getting increasingly
more annoyed now that
Mr Bruce is taking this so seriously.

I then start to hear sirens in the distance,
at first so subtle I don't pay it much attention
until it gets **louder** and **louder**,
until the sound is too loud to ignore,
and it soon becomes clear
that police cars are near.

In seconds, I watch them speeding in
through our school gates and soon
two Norfolk Constabulary squad cars
are screeching to a sharp stop.

Four police officers,
two from each car,
step out looking all stern and serious
and I wonder for a second or two
if they've been called by Mr Bruce
to investigate the whereabouts
of the missing glue.

It's just minutes until the end
of the school day and
there's quite a scene already,
as a stream of students,
let out of class by their teacher a little early,
rush towards the front gate
but then start bunching up
to find out what's going on.

Then through the crowd,
moments later, I see Malachi.
Trousers all baggy and
wearing his black Nike tech fleece hoodie,
walking with two of the officers and
being followed by Mrs Barnham-Broom
and Mr Shaughnessy.

His hands aren't cuffed so
I don't think he's getting arrested
but he's definitely being directed
with a bit of force
towards one of the police cars.

Despite the other teachers'
attempts to calm the situation down
and get the students who
want to watch to go home,
it's all getting a bit chaotic and rowdy,
like the end of a football match when
there's been an unplanned pitch invasion,

with the real risk of someone
getting seriously hurt.

Found it! this girl called Olivia says,
waving the once-missing white stick
around like she's Hermione Granger,
just as one of the police officers
slams the car door shut with Malachi
sat solemnly inside.

ılıı||ıı||ııı

> Bro, it's Malachi, meet at
> Chapelfields at 8. Bandstand,
> near tunnel . . . got something
> for u

> . . . OK yh, hopefully can get
> there then without being bait,
> what happened with the feds
> earlier, is everything OK?

> Just a bunch of dickheads,
> nothing to worry about. See
> you at 8, don't be late.

Shit!

I remember giving Malachi
my number the other week,
obviously, but I hoped he
wouldn't actually message me.
I hoped he wouldn't want to actually meet.

I don't want to go.
I feel the doubt all in my bones,
and god knows what he's gonna say to me,
or try to give to me.
I don't want any part of his
so-called 'business opportunity'.
I don't care if it is actually
all above board and all legal,
like cryptocurrency.
I don't want any part of it,
in all honesty.

Right now, I like it where I am
in the safety and comfort of my room,
propped up by pillows on my bed chilling
watching TikTok clips and Insta stories,
videos of boys from across the country
spitting bars to beats trying to gain a following;
boys like me, in bedrooms chasing their dreams.
I want to carry on watching
Finn Foxell and Knucks videos
on COLORS on YouTube
and imagine it's me.

Of course I've met far worse boys than Malachi
back in London, obviously,
but while living here in Norwich
some part of me inside
feels like it's important to keep him *on* side.
I don't want to seem weak here in this new city.

Anyway, I don't have to do anything he tells me,
I think, as I put on my hoodie,
slide off my sliders and wiggle my feet
into my Air Forces that are not
as fresh-looking as they used to be,
even though I cleaned them just last week
with an old toothbrush and a bit of bleach.

I'll go (reluctantly)
and see what this is all about
and if it's not for me, it's not for me
and I'll tell him so immediately.

I stand for a second or two
in front of the bathroom mirror,
wet-wipe my face,
spray myself down with deodorant,
comb out my hair, chew some gum,
puff my chest out and
take a few deep breaths
and repeat,

**If it's not for me, it's not for me
and I'll tell him so immediately.**

It's just gone seven thirty.
Mum is asleep, snoring on the sofa,
with *EastEnders* about to begin.
She's finished her shift cleaning at
the primary school and
doesn't start her care job till ten.

I walk fast to keep warm and
the quicker I get there,
the quicker I'll be back.
I'm listening to Frankie Stew
at full volume in my headphones.

It's dark but I can see
emo kids in the bandstand,
playing guitar-heavy rock music from
their phones or a
Bluetooth speaker.
The sound isn't coming through clear –
it's all **tinny** and **sizzling**-sounding from here.

It's eight, I'm here on time, but Malachi's late.
I wait, stand awkwardly, hands buried deep
into my pockets, shoulders tense,
bouncing on my toes, by a bench.

I'm shivering, and not cos it's cold (though it is).
The shadows from the trees stain the paths,
branches lurking like long fingers,

and I'm not going to lie, I'm a bit scared,
wondering why I'm here
when deep down inside I don't want to be.

As I check the time on my phone real quick,
I notice the big crack on my screen.
It's gaping more than before,
getting **bigger** and **bigger**, **wider** and **wider**,
slicing the phone into two separate parts,
and in seconds, as I look in between
the grooves, I imagine I'm tumbling in,
falling feet first into the dark,
slipping into the sunken place,
the dirt-encrusted crevice,
with images of Maz and the
43 bus flooding my mind.
Fingers clinging to the side,
clawing and calling for help.

I'm suddenly startled, shaken out of my skin
by something gripping tightly
on to my shoulder; a gloved hand.
'Yes, yes, big man,' Malachi says, giving me a spud.
'You good?' he asks.
I'm obviously not.
I'm shivering all over, stomach in knots,
pretzel-shaped intestines all tight and twisted,
but I don't show too much of my fear
so just gulp then say, 'Yeah.'

There's three of them, Malachi in the middle

and a boy on either side.
The one to his left, the same age or so,
is eating a bag of what looks like
Flamin' Hot Cheetos,
those really dusty twisted ones
that leave orange-red powder
all on your fingers.

'I'm not gonna mess you about –
time is money and all that,' Malachi says,
unironically, clearly taking this
business opportunity really seriously.
'Remember that person who
wanted to speak to you . . .
Well, he wanted me to give you something.

'It's something important that
needs to be handled with care.'

He turns round,
ready to retrieve whatever it is
from the other boy,
but behind Malachi's back
they haven't been paying attention
and don't respond to his cue.
The one who wasn't eating the
Cheetos is in the middle of
doing a Mo Gilligan impression.
'It's like Barbados, it's like Barbados,' he says,
making the other boy,
who still has his mouth full,
crack up laughing.

'Oi, **you lot!** Fix up,'
Malachi addresses them sternly,
clumsily kissing his teeth, clearly
a little pissed off by their silliness
in this apparently serious situation.
And they respond by going quiet
and standing to attention.

Even though I don't know
what I am to be given, this opportunity
feels like some really amateur operation so far.

Then, just as Malachi is about to hand me
whatever it is that he's been given
by the wannabe Mo Gilligan,
there's a flashing light shone
in our direction – a torch? –
and several figures
running towards us from the dark.
Four or five of them at least,
running towards us at speed across the park.

They must have been
watching us the whole time.

It's clear they're feds,
or as Malachi would call them, 'dickheads'.
I can see their reflective clothing and
the little red light glowing from their bodycams.

Frozen with fear for a second,
running through all the potential ramifications
of my actions, my role in this
interrupted transaction,
I soon start to run,
use my Air Forced-feet to flee
as fast I can through the underpass,
past the non-offensive graffiti
on the multicoloured tiles, out the other side,
too scared to look behind.

*Shit! Shit! **Shit!*** I think
as I scarper from the scene at speed,
sprinting out of my skin to get far far away,
still not knowing who, if anyone, is behind me.
*I didn't leave London for **this**.*

I thought I left all this madness behind
but now here I am, miles away from Hackney,
running through an estate,
pelting it through Jenny Lind park
to get away from the feds,
running as fast as I can
without looking back –
just like I did that day
they murdered Maz.

FEBRUARY

**On our way to Shropshire, Leigh nudges me
and says, 'I'm named after one of those.'**

'What, a horse?' I ask, because I can
see lots of them chomping away
on the grass in the many fields we pass
that sit alongside the motorway.

'No, you dickhead. A motorway services.
Don't you dare take the piss, all right,' he says,
as he shuffles closer,
tucks his hair behind his ears,
dips his shoulder a little
and whispers,
'But my full name is Leigh Delamere Gilmour;
Leigh Delamere just happens to be a
motorway services on the M4
between England and Wales,
which is the route my dad took every weekend
to meet my mum back in the day,
when they first started going out.'

I kinda struggle to stop myself laughing.
Imagine being named after a petrol station and
a Costa in the middle of nowhere?
But I manage to hold it in.

We've been travelling for a few hours already,
picking up other students from
outside schools in Cambridge, Coventry,
Wolverhampton and Shrewsbury.

There are fourteen of us altogether and
I'm really glad to have Leigh with me
as we wind our way through the middle of the country,
even though he's probably
even less interested in writing poetry than me
and just pretended he wanted to come,
to keep me company.

I've never been so far up north
and, apart from a camping trip to Lee Valley
one time in Year Six, I don't remember spending a
single night away from home.

I can't lie, I feel a little nervous about it,
not knowing what to expect in the week ahead
and hoping I won't always have to share
my work aloud if I don't want to.
Especially if I decide to write about
Maz or Mum or my little run-in
the other week with the feds.

But that being said,
I'm excited to have time
to work on some new lyrics
for some potential new songs.
As much as it feels uncomfortable sometimes,
I know from previous experience that
it's good to be taken out of your comfort zone
and try new things once in a while.

I scroll through Spotify and Instagram,
listen to little snippets of tracks
on SoundCloud to pass the time,
then scan the feed of some random influencers
and other random profiles, friends of friends,
'careful where I touch' territory, while Leigh
watches an episode of *Drag Race UK*,
a show he's become a bit obsessed with recently.

The minibus finally pulls up,
and I jump out quickly,
headphones round my neck, of course,
desperate to stretch my legs
and breathe in fresh air, having been
cooped up in a little coach
all that time.

I dust down my trackies and
comb out my hair a bit.

I'm impressed with what the building looks like
from the outside, as I
didn't really know what to expect,
but it looks nice in that sort of
old-fashioned, old-white-man house, kind of way.

After being given a Capri-Sun
and a mint-flavoured Club,
we are shown around by the manager, Sophie,

told the rules of the house, the ways in which
we should respect each other and the space,
and follow the health and safety protocols in place.

Everything looks decent.
There's a computer room,
a library with a big round wooden table in the middle
where the writing workshops take place,
a *reading room* (which looks like
a sitting room basically),
and everyone has their own bedroom
with their own en-suite too.

It's proper classy,
like something from a film,
or that thing I saw on ITV the other week,
and we're told by Sophie
that many famous writers have come to
write or teach here through the years,
which is cool.

I can now check out the other students properly,
unlike when we were on the coach.
And I can tell from their trims and kreps
that they're definitely not London folk.

They don't look bad or anything,
it's just there's a very specific London style
that you can clock from a mile away.
There's a very specific London swagger
that you can see almost immediately;
it's the way you have to stand and

the way you strut, how you have to behave,
it's something noticeably different.

They all seem nice but it's too early to tell
if they're cool or not, what their story is,
but we have six days here altogether
for me to find out what everyone is about,
what brings them here,
if that's something they want to share.

It's clear already though, that everyone,
including me, is feeling a bit shy,
not really knowing where to go,
where to look or what to do.

'You support PSG?' one
of the other boys asks me suddenly,
having clocked my tracksuit.
I chat to him for a bit,
this kid in fresh-white Air Forces
similar in style to my pair,
and too much gel in his hair,
who speaks with this weird accent
and tells me he's from Wolverhampton.

Leigh is already talking to some other boy,
laughing with him like they've
known each other for years, running their
fingers along surfaces and skirting boards,
jokingly checking for dust like they do on
that programme on Channel 4, *Four in a Bed*.

But there's this girl . . .
with long curly brown hair
and big brown eyes, walking
around in her own little world.
Taking it all in.

She's got a good vibe, energy, just generally,
and like me, AirPods in – she
must understand the importance
of a good song to get you through certain
potentially awkward situations.

I make a mental note to be brave and,
at some point soon, ask for her name.

I try to make light conversation
with some of the others for a bit,
but after some small talk
I just get this urge to go to my room,
listen to Frankie Stew
and maybe write a few lyrics.

Leigh's still busy making friends with
some boy called Charlie,
so eventually I slink my way upstairs,
to unpack, I say, but actually
it's to plonk down face first
on what will be my bed for the week,
to try and stop the tension building in my head.

ıııı||ı•||ıııı

'So what kinda music you into then?'
I finally pluck up the courage to ask.

Since clocking her earlier,
I've been thinking about her quite a lot already,
the girl with the brown eyes and curly brown hair.
So as we gather in the dining room for dinner,
I finally muster up the confidence
to introduce myself.

Her name is Lana
(I overheard someone say before);
she likes most music
but her favourite artist to listen to at the moment
is someone called Arlo Parks, especially
her debut album, *Collapsed in Sunbeams*.

I think I've come across the name before though
she's not an artist I know much about, to be honest,
but after Lana gives me the lowdown
and recommends some of her best tracks,
I'm definitely intrigued and genuinely mean it
when I tell her that I'm gonna check her out properly.

While we eat, we chat about everything basically,
from fashion to food to football.
She used to play for MK Dons Under-14s
before picking up a nasty knee injury.
She already seems to have made good friends
with some of the others, including twins
Rhianna and Brianna, from Peterborough originally.

But by the end of dinner (vegetarian spaghetti bolognaise)
and dessert (Eton Mess), I already know lots about her:

her name – Lana
her age – 14 (in Year Ten like me)
her city – Milton Keynes
hobbies – music, dancing (ballet), writing poetry, fashion and
football (sometimes goes to watch MK Dons with her dad).

After dessert we start sharing songs we like
off our phones, while some of the others
play Codenames or just chat outside.

Lana and I both like chilled UK hip-hop,
lo-fi conscious rap stuff:
Loyle Carner, Kofi Stone, Ashbeck and Finn Foxell.
Surprisingly, she's not heard of
Frankie Stew or Murkage Dave
but has assured me that she's
gonna give them a listen.

The dining room starts to empty
as some of the others get ready for bed,
but Lana and I agree to play a game of Connect 4,
both giving it heaps of fighting talk,
both claiming to be the best in our respective families
while we set it up and pick our colour –
I go for yellow, she chooses red.

After a tense start,
she wins the first game,

playing smart to entrap me into a two-way win.
I win the second one though,
after she makes a silly mistake,
and with the score tied,
it's best of three, we decide.

We're just setting the last game up as Leigh
pops his head in, wearing a frilly pink hair bonnet,
and says he's heading to bed, giving me
a knowing nod and smile, jutting his head
towards Lana with a teasing stare.

He can't talk.
Ever since arriving here, he's been
spending all his time
laughing and joking with *Charlie*.

The final game goes right down to the wire.
It's all to play for with just a few counters left.
We're both taking it super seriously,
thinking long and hard about our next move
before committing, neither of us wanting to lose
at this late stage of the game.

It looks like it's definitely gonna be a draw
as I plop my yellow counter far right.
A safe move, neither threatening or even that risky,
but I can tell almost immediately
from her facial expression
that she has seen something I haven't, clearly,
and she starts to gloat as she

drops her red into the slot
to snatch the victory.

It takes me a second or two to see it
but then it's clear that she's won.
She sticks out her tongue,
does this little silly dance
and then patronizingly pats my head and says,
'Told you I'd beat you.
Right, I'm going to bed.'

And as she disappears upstairs,
I shout, **'Rematch tomorrow?'**
'Up to you if you want to lose again,'
she responds cheekily,
as the sound of her steps fade.

ᵐᵈ|ᵖᵈ|ᵗᵈᵐ

The first proper day starts with breakfast,
which you have to make yourself.

Most of the others are up already,
but I'm feeling a little too shy to join them,
too worried they'll watch me
not know my way around the kitchen
too closely and judge,
or I'll just get in their way.

I'm not that hungry yet anyway.

Today's weather is good but
the forecast for the rest of the week
is looking bleak, apparently,
says our tutor-in-residence,
Louise, a published poet with an MBE.

She charges in with a full mug of coffee in her hand
and cigarette behind one of her ears,
stands in between the kitchen
and the dining room where myself
and a few others are sat,
and declares energetically
that today's session is going to take place *outside*.

Let's just say the reaction is mixed,
because as nice as this place *is*
(the whole house and the gardens that surround it)
it's been hard to ignore the flies,
from the moment we stepped
out the coach door yesterday.

Getting in my face,
invading my personal space,
not giving anyone a minute's break,
even when you
try to swat them away,
making life unnecessarily
difficult just to go for a walk anywhere,
even with your hood up.

Louise reassures the group *not to worry* and,
once everyone is ready,
we trudge up a little path,
up a little slope that leads
from the back of the house
to this little green spot, and are told
to sit in a semicircle,
all facing Louise on the grass.

But I'm wearing my
brand-new navy PSG tracksuit,
the Air Jordan one that I got for Christmas
and must have taken Mum ages to save for
over several months.
I don't want to get it dirty
on the first proper day here, so instead I
just sort of squat, which is pretty uncomfortable,
but I try to style it out anyway.

To start, Louise gives us a poem called
'Portrait of the Beach'
by South African writer Katharine Kilalea,
and tells us to write a response to it
with the title 'Portrait of Arvon',
exploring the space around us,
taking in the sights and the smells,
making sure to include
every little physical and sensory detail.

We have fifteen minutes,
which feels like enough time as it's a task

that feels kind of similar
to the piece I wrote for Mr Bruce
earlier in the year.

I go and join one of the other boys, **Maher**,
who I was talking to earlier this morning.
He's sat on an old wall under a tree
as he observes this flower closely
that looks like it's just about to bloom.

As he studies it intimately,
he writes down everything he sees.
Not full sentences, just single words:
purple, flower, grow, light, hope,
scrawled along the page,
all *mostly* spelled correctly.

He's from Afghanistan originally and has only
been in this country for a few months.
I sometimes have a little difficulty understanding
everything he says but I always get the gist
and know for a fact I wouldn't be able to
pick up a new language as effortlessly as he has
in the short time he's been here.

'Here is different from home,' he says,
looking lovingly out on to the landscape.
'Afghanistan today is bad, really dangerous,'
he says while making a bomb explosion
gesture with his hands
and obviously I've never been to Asia,

but in a strange sort of way I understand
what it can be like living with the constant fear
that something could go wrong at any minute.

Even though I've basically only just met him,
I'm in awe of his bravery and positivity,
despite all the horrible things he has seen,
and now being here in the UK,
without any family.

I enjoy chatting to him,
listening to his stories
about his life back home and
the horrors he experienced
travelling to get here as a refugee,
a journey that saw him travel through over
a dozen countries – Iran, Turkey,
Serbia, Hungary, Germany, then into France,
scrambling into the back of a lorry.

Leigh's so far been spending a lot of time
with Charlie, which makes me happy to see.
They're clearly getting on and have
hit it off already.

I leave Maher to it and try to pick something
specific I can focus on for this activity.
I struggle to get into any kind of rhythm at first,
and while I try and think of
something I can write about,

I spy Lana, who is a little below me,
sitting on a bench in the walled garden,
writing away busily.

I decide to have a go focusing on
something in the distance instead,
and I think I can see,
as I look towards the hills,
a small wooden barn,
tin-roofed and tired-looking,
near a little lake.

And behind the barn,
I can see these great big trees
swaying softly like they've
had too much to drink.

After fifteen minutes,
Louise tells us all
to come together again
and I decide to sit down
on the grass properly,
like the rest of the group,
not worried about dirtying my bottoms any more,
because actually when you deep it,
it doesn't really matter,
not when you're here
in the middle of the countryside
in the middle of nowhere.
It's just too beautiful to care.

Lana offers to share what she's written
and Louise is delighted at the idea of
hearing her words, and as she
starts reading her piece,
it's clear that somehow she's
managed to produce magic
in just a matter of minutes.
Her poem is absolutely amazing and
I'm in complete awe of her . . . words.

In between the morning
and afternoon sessions of the day,
there is a fifteen-minute break to use the
toilet or get a snack or hot drink,
and as we make our way back down the slope
into the kitchen, I go up to Lana
just to tell her how much
I really enjoyed her portrait piece.

I can tell she feels a bit embarrassed
and shy to be complimented,
but also clearly appreciates
too that I've made the effort to share
how her poem made me feel.
And I'm relieved when she casually
offers to make me a tea, as she
makes herself one confidently,
knowing already where everything is.
I accept her invitation gratefully,
desperate to have something warm
at last inside my belly.

'How do you manage to get so much power
in your work?' I ask.
'Like it's so mad that the words
you use just sound so deep and meaningful.
I can't lie, I'm still thinking about
certain images from your piece right now.'

She blushes, smiles, looks down nervously
at her sliders and wiggles her toes.
'Not sure really – I read a lot, I suppose,
my dad works at the Open University,
teaching history,
so there's always been lots of books in the house,
and when I get bored of playing
on my phone or watching telly,
I just sit on the sofa and read.'

She tells me she's just finished reading this book
called *The Crossing* by Manjeet Mann
and says it inspired her to write
a poem about how all that's going on currently
was making her angry, like the
awful treatment of Rwanda-bound refugees.

'*The Crossing* made me cry, because it's like
these poor people, sometimes children, have come
from heavily bombed war-torn countries,'
she says, no longer looking shy.

'They've lost their homes and members
of their families and here in the UK, we're like,

Nah, we don't care.
Go back to the dangerous country you came from,
or even worse, a country you've
probably never even heard of before.
*You're not welcome here, **we're full**.*

'It's ironic really
that Britain has the cheek to call itself **Great**,
when it feels it's OK to treat fellow humans
in a not-Great way.

'You **have** to read it, Ronny –
let me go get it for you,
you can borrow it for the week,'
she says, as she skips
out the kitchen and rushes upstairs
before I even have the chance to reply.

When she comes back less than a minute later
and hands it over to me,
I study the book's bright orange cover,
with two illustrated teenagers
looking away from each other:
one Black boy, one white girl,
and think it looks pretty good actually.

'What are you passionate about?' she asks,
a big question coming out of the blue
as I flick through the book absent-mindedly.

I need some time to think about a
question of this degree,

but after a pause I say,
'Music, of course, but football mainly,
all of the politics around it
has interested me lately,
especially like racism and
the whole **"taking the knee"**;
and the things some users post
about Black footballers on
social media, especially like what happened
when England lost to Italy
in the final of the Euros
and those three Black players
missed their penalties.'

'Use that,' she says to me.
'Use that fury. Use that anger.
Outrage and creativity
often go hand in hand. Trust me.'

We chat some more over our hot drinks
in the dining room and we
decide that one day soon hopefully,
we will work on a sort of protest song together,
a powerful one about the state of society.
We'll write the lyrics and put it to a good beat,
get someone to shoot a video
and someone else to design the single's front cover.

ılı||ıı||ııı

Up in my room later that evening,
I start thinking about what Lana said

and type some lines on my phone.
I try to think about Rashford, Sancho and Saka,
but as hard as I try to concentrate,
all I can think about is Lana.

STRANGE FEELING

this is a strange feeling I've not felt before
I say nice things wanting you to believe it
I say you're a perfect portrait but you cannot see it

this is a strange feeling I've not felt before
I say that I need you and hope you know I mean it
you say your heart has been dirtied,
so I promise to deep-clean it

picture perfect night
see our future in those perfect brown eyes
I'm there to check if you're all right
see these feelings taking off,
watch them take flight
somewhere we've not been before
watching our dreams come alive

what's the point, it ain't easy
the way you make me feel,
feel my heart, it's freezing
I deserve to feel a way
with somebody that will stay
but the way you look at me I can't believe it

I want this feeling to last forever
I look at you and see less days alone
I see a future, mask off, just you and me
skin to **skin**, **body** to **body**, **bone** to **bone**

I say that you're special but you don't believe
the fact that I need someone who's right for me
the right one came along so effortlessly
in the shape of you, a **GOAT**, Lionel Messi

feel the music of these words through your soul
you know I won't ever leave you on your own
played my cards, my true colours all shown
now you'll finally know I won't
leave you hurting, your heart or your soul

this is a strange feeling I've not felt before
I say nice things wanting you to believe it
I say you're a perfect portrait but you cannot see it

We do our morning pages, of course,
to start today's session but then next
Louise gives us another poem from the poet
from yesterday – Katharine Kilalea.
It's another 'Portrait' poem,
but this one's called 'Portrait of Our Death'.

I like it a lot.
It's deep how the speaker describes

the moments she and her friends nearly died
after the car they're in
loses grip at the end of a cliff.
There are so many lines that hit hard;
it's a dramatic but hopeful little story
written in the form of poetry.

Louise prompts us to write a creative response,
a short piece about a time we were scared.
A dramatic, heart-stopping experience.
An occasion where our whole life
flashed before our eyes.

'If writing from personal experience
is too triggering for this activity,' Louise says,
'you can make up a completely imaginary
character or maybe even an alias,
so it sort of resembles what
happened in your life but
is retold by someone new.'

I think about writing something
that did actually
happen to me,
like that time I could have drowned
in Britannia Leisure Centre
near our old flat in Hackney.

But I'm more drawn to writing about
what happened to Maz
for the first time since writing that

long statement at the police station
that fateful day in May.

I'm tempted to creatively
note down all the details of the tragedy,
of being in the wrong place,
on the wrong day,
to look at the wrong person in their face,
and for some stupid reason,
and my cowardly behaviour,
Maz was made to pay.

I start writing a few lines, call it:
'Portrait of Your Death',
but something doesn't feel right.
My stomach feels all tight and knotted,
head hurts too, feels all squashed and clotted
and my eyes start to sting,
and it's soon clear why.
Thinking about what happened to Maz
all those months ago, is making me cry.

I can't do it, hurts too much still, still too raw.
I'm rushing towards the workshop door.
Leigh shouts after me,
but I'm already charging at full speed
down the main steps,
tears spilling down my cheeks.

As usual, today's session
starts with morning papers,
which is basically just an opportunity
to free-write for five minutes or so,
'warm up our brains and loosen our wrists',
as Louise likes to say.

She starts to play
a song and we just have to listen,
take it all in, and then,
as the song slows to a stop,
start writing down whatever
comes into our head.

As Louise presses PLAY on her iPhone
and the song starts to play through
her Bluetooth speaker,
Lana's face suddenly starts to light up bright
and she begins whispering excitedly
to Brianna next to her.

I think it's a song she likes.
It must be by the artist she loves
– Arlo Parks.

It sounds good: soulful and deep
with a really good beat,
definitely something I would
listen to in my own time.

As soon as the song comes to an end,
Lana begins writing straightaway,
eager since the start of the track
to jot down a few lines.

I, on the other hand, am struggling.
Struggling to find the right words,
things that sound at least
a bit good even for a first draft,
things that would suit the tone of the music,
something Lana might be impressed by,
and as Louise tells us to finish our last line
and put our pens down,
I end up writing pure gibberish
sentences that sound too simple
or just don't really make sense.

Sitting opposite me though, I can see
Lana has written what looks like a whole poem
super quickly and is keen,
but in a shy sort of way,
to share what she's come up with
among the rest of the group.

DREAMS

Life is coming out the other side
of a difficult time,
a long dark tunnel somewhere unfamiliar,
and still feeling alive.

Full of joy like
a message from a loved one
a seat at the table
a voice that gets listened to
a platform to be understood
a safe walk home
a saving grace in the
form of a smiling face
guiding you to safety

so in the darker times
remember the days
when your dreams
kept you awake,
this is just the beginning
of the journey to make
them all come true one day.

The whole room is amazed as she says
her last line and sits back down.

It's clear she's a natural poet,
a special kind of storyteller.
It's just so impressive how she manages to
conjure up this vivid imagery so easily,
painting a picture of a scene effortlessly
so it's almost like we're actually there,
in this world that she's created,
using all the right words
that just roll off the tongue and

make you feel something deep down,
in through the ears and right down to the heart.

'Wow!' Louise exclaims and makes us all give
Lana a second well-deserved round of applause.
'That was incredible, Lana, incredible!'

For the next activity, Louise comes round
with this little dingy beige sack
she calls her *swag bag*.
'With hundreds of different handwritten
words inside,' she claims, completely
weird and random ones like,
Joyously, **Ketchup**, **Manchester** and **Inflamed**.

She tells us to grab a small handful
and spread them out on the table,
so I plunge my hand in
and pick out nine or ten.

Then Louise comes round with a bunch
of old newspapers and magazines
and instructs us to cut out
one figure from them.
It could be a fashion model,
a cartoon character or an animal –
just someone or something we would want to
write about for the activity to follow.

I get to work, begin to try and **make magic**
as Lucas would say in our sessions back at school
on a Friday.

The character I've chosen
is a Black man from *GQ*
covered in tattoos,
snapped at some kind of music festival.

I write **a word**.
Then another **one**.
Then another **two**.

Soon I have **a sentence**.
Then **a paragraph**.
Then **a page**.

Before I know it, I'm deep into the activity . . .

The time is up, almost too quickly,
and I know I could have probably
even written more but as I skim over the words
that I've produced in the time, I know already
I've done the first piece this week
that I'm actually really proud of.

BLACK IS A CLENCHED FIST

Black is a clenched fist
not used for fighting
but as a show of strength
like hauling someone up
who has fallen down
and is floundering, about to drown

Black is a party
where everyone is invited
and the only restriction that applies
is that you must know how to candy-slide

Black is the cat
slinking through the flap.
The neighbour's TV is blaring,
they've bought a fancy new soundbar.
Black is that, everything and more.

Black is not stop-and-search
and permanent exclusions –
it's the jiggling of hips
and Vaseline on the lips
and the whining of waists
till the sun goes down
and you are tired but picked up
and taken home by that same clenched fist from line one
that will always be there for you.

ᴵᴵᴵᴵ|ᴵᴵᴵ||ᴵᴵᴵᴵ

Our guest performer for the week
goes by the name Testament.
'He's a rapper, beatboxer, scriptwriter and singer,'
Sophie says, reading his bio from a sheet of paper.

He's a man in his early forties, I'd say,
who wears denim baggy jeans
and skateboarder-style trainers.

It takes him a little while to get set up,
plug in his microphone and speakers and stuff,
but after like twenty minutes he's
ready and so are we,
sat on the sofas in the sitting room,
not fully sure what to expect or
what exactly he's going to do.

I'm sitting in between Lana and Maher,
while unsurprisingly Leigh
is snuggled up with Charlie.

The music begins
and Testament starts turning little knobs
and pushing buttons on his loop machine,
and then after a little while
starts performing properly
and I'm blown away almost immediately,
watching in awe,
completely compelled by his charismatic energy.

Somehow he makes these mad beats
just by using his mouth
that are as good as, if not better,
than beats made on some fancy
MacBook Pro in some studio.
It's not quite MK The Plug or M1onTheBeat,
these are not grime or drill sounds,
but super special in their own
old-school hip-hop way.

It's like nothing I've ever heard before in the flesh
and when his first performance is finished
we all applaud really loudly.

Then, after a bit of a brief intro,
telling us some of the backstory
and context of what it means
to be a mixed-race man
growing up in South London,
he goes on to perform this poem called 'Harmony',
about having a Black mum from Ghana,
and a white dad from this country,
and I can tell, see from the glassiness of her eyes
that Lana is particularly moved by it,
and is now also under his spell.

Then he says he's going to try
a little freestyle and, to prove it's entirely
made up on the spot,
he asks the group for completely
random words for him to include.

'Burna Boy!' shouts Ameno instantly.
'That's technically two but it'll do,' Testament says,
as he whips out a Biro from his back pocket
and finds a bit of scrap paper to
scribble the suggestions down on.

'ABBA!' shouts Charlie.
Testament writes that down too and says,
'I can detect a musical theme emerging here.'

I shout out **'Ronaldo!'**
'Louise!' shouts Louise with a glint
in her eye and then a wink.

Maher says **'Cricket.'**
Brianna cheekily says **'Orange,'**
Rhianna cheekily says **'Purple,'**
prompting Testament to give them
both a knowing look.

'Frankie Stew!' shouts Lana.
'I know that's technically two too,'
she adds and then looks to her left at me,
knowing I would be proper pleased.
She confessed earlier that she's
been listening to his stuff
since my recommendation and how
she now likes their music as much as I do.

After a minute or two and more ideas
from the rest of the group,
Testament now has over
fourteen words and phrases to include.

He starts off a new beat
on his little machine
and then flattens out the list
and begins thinking of
clever ways to mix the words given
into some kind of original song.

Despite our best attempts to pick words
that would really challenge him,
Testament manages to make it look easy
and include them all into the rap pretty cleverly.

All of us are sufficiently
impressed by the end,
more than sufficiently actually.
Properly gobsmacked.

After an incredible evening
of incredible music
showcased in a wide range
of experimental ways,
I know for sure,
even more now than before,
that some kind of creative
is what I want to be.
I know I want to play around with words
and amaze people watching,
causing a similar reaction to what
Testament has just had with me.

To top off an excellent night,
just as everyone else crowds around him
to chat a bit more and take selfies,
a tired Lana rests her head
on my shoulder unexpectedly,
her curly brown hair tickling
the bottom of my chin,

which, I can't deny, makes me
hysterically happy.

···||·|·||···

We've been waiting in the workshop for
like ten minutes or so,
and Maher's still not here.

Which is strange because he's been
on time every day this week,
in fact, he's usually been early,
but right now, at this big
round wooden table
where he's supposed to be,
he's nowhere to be seen.

'Perhaps he's still asleep,' someone says.
'Maybe he's praying somewhere,'
is another idea.
'Maybe he's gone on a walk.'
Could be . . .
but with the rain coming down
outside, hard and heavy,
that seems highly unlikely.

I know he's really enjoyed being here
but also that it's not been easy.
All week so far, he's been
watching little bits of news
on his phone, hoping he might catch a little

glimpse of his mum,
who's still back in Afghanistan,
and at risk, in more ways than one,
because of the Taliban.

But he usually can't watch the shots of
what's been going on for long
just in case he does eventually see
something really really wrong.

'Has anyone got his number?' Louise asks.
And even though I'm sure I don't
as I check my phone to see if I might do,
I notice I've got a text from Malachi:

> Really sorry, bro, things got a bit
> sticky back in the Chapelfields
> when it wasn't supposed to . . .

Nice of him to apologize.
I'll reply, I think, as soon as we find Maher.

Louise doesn't seem too worried yet.
She's been teaching at Arvon for years,
has seen it all, she's told us,
from blossoming romances to runaways,
and remains calm and unflustered
as she announces that today's session will

start a little later than planned, and suggests
we all split up and look for our friend.

So Louise, me, Lana, Leigh, Charlie, Brianna,
Rhianna, Ameno, Majid, Wolverhampton Will
and the rest of the group too
go in search of him,
all still pretty much half asleep
in our socks, slippers and sliders.

We search everywhere but he's
not in the computer room,
the little snug or the kitchen,
not in the office or any of the bedrooms.
We've looked under everywhere and
behind everything and he's definitely
not in the house.

Sophie suggests to Dan,
the caretaker here –
who wears skinny jeans,
braces and high-top Dr. Martens –
to have a look in the surrounding woods,
so he straightaway swaps
his Docs for his wellies,
dons his raincoat and heads outside.

And then, as everyone starts to
get more anxious and worried,
out of nowhere, like a slap
on the head, it hits me.
I know just where Maher might be.

I don't say anything to the others as I rush out
the main entrance and into the pouring rain.
I clamber down the front steps,
taking them two at a time,
and sprint round the back of the house,
my sliders smacking the slippery
wet paving stones.

I run up the slope, my socks getting
more soaked by the second,
white a minute ago, now brown,
sodden and mulchy,
then rush across the grassy
patch where we all sat the other day.
In the distance I see,
still getting wet despite sitting
under the canopy of a big tree,
a figure wearing a black hoodie,
sat on the old wall
overlooking the flower garden.

He's hunched over something,
something he's gripping proper
tight in his hands, and
as I get closer I see it's
some kind of book,
orange in colour it looks like.
The pages are all wet.

As I shuffle closer to the tree,
to try and stop myself getting
drowned by the downpour

by huddling under its leaves,
I can see it's the book that Lana
was talking about before,
the one that's about the journey of a refugee –
Manjeet Mann's *The Crossing*.
I must have accidentally
left it in the kitchen after she gave it to me.

I can see Maher's face clearly now.
His eyes are wet, red and puffy, and
it's not just because of the rain.
He's been crying and before I even ask,
I know that he's been
thinking about his mum in Afghanistan again.

I can see the worry flood his face
and all I can do in that moment, as
the rain pours down heavy,
small splashes gradually
becoming big puddles,
is give him the tightest hug
with both my arms and suddenly
in the cold, all I feel is warmth.
Warmth and love.

ᵗᵗᵗ||ᵗᵗ||ᵗᵗᵗ

As part of the retreat we all get to
have a one-to-one tutorial with Louise.
It's a chance to talk through
some of my pieces so she

can suggest ways to make
them better and just improve generally.

It's also an opportunity
to talk about which piece we
might choose to perform
at the end-of-residency
showcase tomorrow.

'How's it been going this week?'
Louise asks me, as she
shifts and shuffles to get
comfortable in her seat.

'Good,' I reply;
'really good actually.
I've definitely got more confident
as the week has gone on, and
I think I've written some pretty decent pieces.
It's surprised me just how much I've enjoyed it really.
In fact, I've been trying to learn this new one
I've been working on, off by heart.'

She seems impressed by this aim,
pulls a little **'Is that you, Ronny, yeah?'**
face and says of course it can be done,
as she puts her reading glasses on,
thumbs in the passcode
of her iPad and begins loading up a
video on YouTube.

The first video is of George the Poet,
a performance called 'It Was Written'.
Not a video I've seen before,
but it's clear to see that he
has this mad flow that suits
the tone he's trying to convey,
for the powerful message he's trying to relay.

'The way you deliver your piece will be key,
obviously,' Louise advises me,
and suggests using little gestures
and little subtle actions
so that I can remember
particular words at particular times –
especially the lines that rhyme.

'Every poet does it,' she says,
'and actors too – it's true!
There are always helpful things
like that you can do
to help get the message of the piece through.'

And Louise says to ensure I give it
all my energy and that she'll be sat there
rooting for me. And in just fifteen minutes
with her I'm feeling so inspired and
can't wait already for
everyone to hear what I've come up with,
to show them what I can do.

We've all been building up
to this for the last few days –
the chance to perform some
of our best poems or stories
we've been working on during our stay.

In the living room of the house,
the space with all the comfy sofas,
coffee table and books,
some of the others have picked flowers
and decorated the space around the 'stage',
using posies and neatly cut people paper chains.
It actually does look pretty cool, to be fair.

Louise gets ready to watch,
nestled in on one of the sofas
opposite the makeshift stage
with her usual cup of coffee,
eagerly anticipating what everyone has
come up with this week.
She's dressed for the occasion too,
done her hair and put on a nice smartish suit.

We're all set, more or less ready to begin,
but someone is missing:
Leigh.

Where is he? Everyone's here except him.
Come to think of it, I haven't actually
seen him since, like, this afternoon.
I assumed he was sleeping

or something but he can't be
in bed still, no way,
he's known all week that we
have to perform today.

As I start to rack my brain,
Sophie comes in and assures the group
that Leigh is on his way,
just 'dealing with something' upstairs,
which sounds strange and vague.

We all agreed earlier that Ameno should be
tonight's host, the designated MC,
and have the job of introducing
all the performers before they go
to the front to share their piece.

First, to begin the evening,
he gives a little speech
about how much he has enjoyed the week
and how grateful he is
to have had this opportunity
to meet everyone,
the other writers from all over the country,
including the tutor, Louise,
before he then invites the first performer
to stand up and read out their work.

Ameno retrieves a little scrap
of paper from his back pocket
with the line-up of readers scribbled on it

and says, 'First up to read is . . .'
his face all scrunched up and baffled, as he
looks up again and starts to
peer around the room.
'Where's Leigh?'
he says, looking at Charlie
and then at me.

Neither of us know.

'Leigh!' Ameno shouts semi-loudly.
'Oh, Leigh!' he says again as he
starts to look under
the sofa cushions comically.

'Where are you? It's your time to read!'
Charlie is clearly as baffled as me and
gets his phone out to send him a message,
when suddenly the door opens a little and
a sequin-gloved hand
snakes its way through into view,
first one set of wiggling fingers,
then two.

It's Leigh's hand, obviously,
but as he sidles into the room properly, he
looks even more beautiful than usual.
In fact, so beautiful, he's
like a different person completely.
He's wearing a dress and make-up
and a wig and high heels.

He's wearing pink nail varnish on his toes too.
He looks kind of . . . **incredible**.

Everyone is mesmerized,
struggling to take their
eyes off this glamorous individual, and then
Lana starts yelling, **'Go, Leigh!'**
But Leigh replies abruptly,
sticks out his hand as if to stay STOP.
'No. Call me *Miss De La Mare*,'
he insists dramatically,
turning to me and winking.

Miss De La Mare stands in the centre,
clears their throat, fairy lights glowing bright
on the mantelpiece, and then
starts reading their piece off their phone
that they retrieved from their little handbag.

The tone is a bit different from
how Leigh speaks usually
but it works, it all works –
the look, the style,
the heels, the voice.
There isn't a word that
feels out of place.

It's a prose poem piece about identity
and being free to be who you want to be.
They end with a line from Dean Atta's
The Black Flamingo: 'I am the fairy
finding my own magic.' Perfect.

Everyone applauds,
me and Charlie super proudly
but Louise stands up and
starts clapping **extra loudly**.
It looks like she's laughing
and crying at the same time.

It's Lana's turn next.

As Lana recites her words off by heart,
like a seasoned performer who's been
playing the part of a professional poet for years,
once again, I'm completely mesmerized.

As I hear her perform,
it's like there's no one else
in the room apart from just me and her,
and I find myself closing my eyes,
imagining her reciting her lines
just to me . . . privately.

Everyone is clapping –
she's done it again,
produced her usual
high standard of magic.

It's my turn next and I've decided to share
a new piece I've been working on –
this sort of hybrid thing,
a song of sorts, with a chorus and
a little bit of singing,
mixed with these really poetic lines,

because for the first time really,
this week has made me
realize there's lots of similarities
between rapping and spoken word,
song lyrics and poetry.

It's called 'Stuck' and still very rough.

I get up and I wasn't really
feeling nervous before
but I'm suddenly all **jittery**.
There's only, like, fourteen others
in the room, including Louise,
but it's kind of scary standing here
just about to pour my heart out
in front of everybody.

My legs feel **weak** and **unsteady**
and my hands are **trembling**.
The paper with my piece on
is **shaking** in my hands.

I know what I want to say
and how I want to say it
but as I begin it doesn't seem to be
coming out right – it's clear
I haven't quite perfected the delivery.

But as I stutter, I look towards Lana
and her expression is
all warm and encouraging,

like a hot mug of Milo,
giving a little smile
that's enough to feel like a hug,
and then I remember
some of the lines from her 'Dreams' poem
earlier in the week:

> a saving grace in the
> form of a smiling face
> guiding you to safety

and that's enough to keep me going,
to stop me from crumbling completely.

I stumble once or twice more but I carry on
and with each line I recite
I'm starting to find my flow,
starting to feel less shivery,
starting to feel like I'm smashing it lyrically,
and manage to end it strongly.

Everyone claps, which is a relief.
After a shaky start, you know what?
I think I did all right.
I did kind of good.

Maher is next and before he
makes his way to the front, he asks me
to use my phone to film him while he reads.
Something I should have done
for my own performance

come to think of it, so
Mum could see me
performing for the first time.

Like I did when I started my piece,
he stumbles a little, here and there
on the odd word, but to me and,
I'm sure, to everybody,
it sounds absolutely perfect,
perhaps the best piece
I've ever heard, and everyone,
including a very tearful Louise clearly,
but especially me, is so immensely
proud of him.

For the final day,
Louise leads us all on a walk
to the top of one of the hills
that surround the house.

One last chance to make memories.

But on the way up, she says
the one rule is we're not allowed to speak,
not even a single word.
Instead just write down any
interesting things we see
and by the time we reach the summit,
turn it into a creative piece.

Because it's been raining most of the week
and much of the grass outside
is still sodden and wet,
Louise suggests we
borrow some wellies to wear,
which fills us, particularly me,
with despair.

The idea of donning some dirty decades-old
second-hand boots horrifies me, in all honesty,
but Lana just puts them on without fuss,
so I follow her lead.
If it's good enough for her,
then they're good enough for me,
and I sit on the bench by the front door and
wiggle the wellie on effortlessly.

Off we trek with our notebooks and pens,
and as we slowly weave our way up,
making the most of the imposed silence,
I decide to play the clown and start
showing off to Lana
by doing silly TikTok dances,
and a bit of old-school dabbing.

The view is pretty cool
and even if we weren't instructed to stay silent,
I don't really know what I would say anyway,
because the view from the top
of the hills, the wildlife, the sky,
sort of takes my breath away.

I look at Lana then,
and Lana looks at me,
but still neither of us say a word,
stunned by the beauty of the scene
and, as a pair of large birds circle above us,
our longing stares turn into loving smiles.

Now allowed to speak,
we share our last few words of the week
stood in a semicircle round Louise,
and one by one we begin reading out
a few lines from what we saw
that has now formed our final creative piece.

The perfect last task to capture
an incredible experience over the last few days.

I challenge Lana to a race
back down the winding hill
towards the house, which I instantly
regret because her wellies fit more snugly
than mine and she speeds ahead to win easily.

I tell her I let her win, obviously,
when the truth is she's just generally
faster and fitter than me,
and by some distance too.

꜒꜐꜒꜐꜒

Before we set off, meaning
a long trip back to Norwich for me and Leigh,
we're given little packed lunches for the journey:
a tuna or cheese sandwich, an apple,
some juice and a KitKat Chunky.

As some of the others double-check
they haven't forgotten anything upstairs
in their bedrooms, there's just enough time
for me and Maher to have a final chat
before we have to go.

'Maher, I'm gonna miss you, my friend,' I say,
going in for a hug.
His response is a big beaming
smile and a comforting arm round my neck.
As the days have gone on,
like all of us in some way,
he's grown in confidence and is much chattier
than when we first got here on our first day.

I tell him that we must
make sure to stay in touch

and then we get talking about TikTok
and cricket, his favourite sport,
and he is keen to show me him in action
back home in Afghanistan, a video
that was posted online a little while ago
of him doing an impressive fast bowl.
He tells me the video has thousands of views,
and basically went viral.

But as he goes into his
pocket to get out his phone,
he suddenly stops
and remembers that it's
'Dead, upstairs'.

'Where's your charger?' I ask.
He shakes his head, looks down.
'I forgot to bring.'

'How many days has it been dead for?'
I then ask him.

After he thinks about it for a second or two,
'Since Wednesday,' he says, and nods.

It's Saturday now, meaning he's gone
three whole days without a charged phone,
which isn't the worst thing in the world, obviously,
but for Maher means he hasn't had the chance
to watch the news clips
like he was watching religiously
at the beginning of the week.

It probably explains why we couldn't get
a hold of him the day he ran off in the rain.

'Why did you not say?'
I ask, as I get out my powerpack
from the front pocket of my bag.

He's clearly very grateful
to have at least an hour of power
for the journey, as he plugs his phone in.
But the fact he never asked before
makes me a little sad.
He literally could have
asked any one of us and we
would have let him
borrow it for the whole week
if he needed it – that's how much
Maher is loved here by everybody.

As I pack my last bits away,
making sure I have my house keys,
my wallet and my little Vaseline,
I can't quite believe that we're leaving today.
Something I never thought I would ever say.

I'm feeling gutted that I
might not see many of these
faces again, these
new friends I've made.

I know, having left good friends back in London,
that's just how life is sometimes.
Losing touch is just
one of those things that happen
as you get older, as sad as that is.

I really didn't think Arvon was going
to be all that good at first,
when I initially agreed to come here –
even when I arrived, hopped out
of the minibus for the first time.
But it's probably been
one of the best weeks of my life.
Genuinely.

On the way back to Norwich,
like we did at the beginning of the week,
we stop off at various points along the way.

Just outside Coventry,
Leigh says goodbye to Charlie,
gives him a long strong hug and
then waggles his finger in his face flirtatiously
and says, 'Make sure you DM me,'
followed by a little peck on the cheek.
They kiss again – on the lips, quickly –
before Leigh is instructed back to his seat
by the driver, so we can continue the journey.

At Milton Keynes, Lana gives me one last hug
and just before she lets go,

squeezes in a little kiss too,
which entertains the rest of the group,
who say in unison
(orchestrated by Leigh, predictably),
a combination of **awwwwws** and **ooooooos**,
making me embarrassed but also more than a
little excited inside too.

My heart feels all warm and fuzzy and
strange, knowing how lucky I am
to have met her this week, and
as soon as she is out of sight
and the bus pulls out and away,
and heads back towards the motorway,
I already can't wait to see her again.

ONE MORE DAY

**Lana, you made me see the light
I wonder if you were dazzled by it too?
I wonder if you would stay one more night
I wonder if you like that idea as much as I do**

**Effortlessly dancing over puddles,
in your Nike Air Forces and white Nike socks
pulled all the way up,
your brown curls poking out the hood
of your North Face puffer**

**You carry the fire and flair
of some intrepid explorer on a quest to**

discover everything that's out there
The rain this week didn't wash away your
thirst to keep learning,
to keep growing,
soaring sky high till we all see
the early streaks of sunlight

You make me want to go back and write again
and even though I know we can't stay
I wish I could return with you and for this not to end
even if it was just for one more day

MARCH

It's Friday night and usually
I'd just be at home
chilling and listening to music
or watching reels and stuff,
maybe even posting a snippet
or two of new material of my own.

But Leigh, well, his dad actually,
has managed to get tickets for the
Norwich City game at Carrow Road,
so obviously, free tickets are free tickets.
So when he texted me earlier,
I said, *Yeah, OK, I'll go.*

Leigh's dad works for the car company Lotus,
one of the team's sponsors, Leigh told me,
so he often gets tickets,
sometimes in the posh bit
next to the chairman and directors,
but as this is a last-minute thing,
I think we're just sitting in the
normal seats for tonight's game.

It's my first time seeing
my new home city play.
Actually, it's my first time
going to a proper football game.
Mum has always said that one day when she had
the money, or won the lottery
(which she doesn't even play),
that she would take me to Old Trafford to see

United, but that dream looks less and less likely
than it did when she
first said it on my tenth birthday.

She was actually a bit worried
when I asked her if I could go tonight.
She thinks football fans are thugs
just looking for a fight but when I told her that
Leigh's coming with me, she reluctantly agreed
that I could go as long as I was extra careful,
that we stick together and I'm not ever left alone.

Leigh and I meet up on Unthank Road,
outside a closed Caffè Nero.
Leigh wears a retro home shirt
under a black leather jacket
with little rhinestones studded on the lapel,
and bright yellow flared corduroy trousers
that are so wide at the bottom
it kind of looks like a skirt,
with his dark green moon boots.

Despite all the layers I've got on,
I'm still feeling the cold
as we follow the crowd of football fans
walking up Prince of Wales Road.
It's already quite busy out
with rowdy drunk people
wanting to have fun on a Friday night.

Outside a club called Sugar and Spice,
two burly bouncers,

tattoos on their hands, fingers
and all round their necks,
are about to start their shift.

There's a homeless man sitting on the floor
outside Tesco Express, his scruffy beanie
all wonky on his head,
holes in his Slazenger trainers,
with his dirty palms outstretched,
asking passers-by,
if they have any spare change.

I don't have anything at all
to give and Leigh
is busy on his phone,
probably WhatsApping Charlie,
judging by the wide smile on his face.

I catch a glimpse of this poor man's eyes, see
his desperation, sense his misery
and can't help but feel sorry
for him as I imagine what his life
might be like, living on these cold streets.
No real home, waking up in the doorway
of Primark with nowhere to go,
not knowing where his
next meal might come from,
not knowing who to trust,
trying to get by day by day,
wanting help, only just surviving on his own.

We get to the stadium,
which is actually pretty cool,
I think, as we enter through the turnstiles
and find our seats. We are really close
to the away fans who have completely
filled their section and are already standing and
singing at the top of their lungs, long before
the game has even kicked off.

They're **so loud**,
and Leigh and I are just, like,
a few seats away as they chant
song after song,
which, from what I can tell,
are *sometimes* quite witty
but nearly always offensive.

They soon start singing one about
me and Leigh specifically, yelling,
We can see you holding hands!
just because we happen to be
sitting next to each other.
Leigh is unbothered,
takes it in his stride,
pouts his lips, and swishes
his hair with pride.

Thankfully only a small handful
of the stand join in
and the song peters out
before it really begins.

They barely even watch the game,
which Norwich eventually win two-nil,
but even though I wore all the layers
I could without looking too silly –
long johns under my jeans and long sleeves –
it's still so cold, I can't even feel my fingers
by the full-time whistle.

My feet are frozen as we
shuffle out the stadium and back
towards the centre of the city.

Stumbling out of the Irish pub
on the corner, a large group
of women wearing rose-gold sashes
and tutus, on a hen night it seems,
start singing Beyoncé's 'Single Ladies'
really loudly to the bride-to-be.

And as we go past the kebab shops,
with rotating skewers of meat
catching the artificial light,
there's something going on up ahead;
sounds like some kind of fight.
There's an eruption of noise,
a brawl of sorts,
that's sounding far from polite.

There's a big group of men, or boys,
it's hard to tell from here, four or five of them,
all surrounding a guy on the floor,
shouting and swearing proper aggressively.

Maybe Mum was right –
going to football on a Friday night
wasn't the best idea after all.

Most of the other people, probably
about to start their night,
or who've had a few too many pints already,
just walk past and ignore what's going on,
having a quick look before heading into
one of the many bars and clubs.

As Leigh and I edge closer, I can clearly see
the main characters of this dramatic scene.
We stop just short, but even from
down the road I can still see that they're
ganging up on the same homeless man
that caught my eye from before.
The one that was sitting on the floor.

The main perpetrator
wearing a Palm Angels turtleneck
is shouting furiously at the man,
but it's only as we get closer that I can start to
really make out some of the words
of their heated conversation.
It sounds like they know each other in some way
and there's some kind of history,
some unfinished business
needing to be sorted out between them.

Even if we wanted to, there's nothing we can do –
there's, like, five of them and it's only us two.

The man is pleading with the ringleader.
'Please, I'm sorry, don't hurt me.'
'You think I'm a mug?' the tough guy says
as he pulls back his leg
and boots him in the chest.
I can see a Rambo knife
poking out of his back pocket.

'I'll get you the money,'
the man on the floor promises.
'I'll have it soon, I swear.
Just need another day or two.'

'Am I a joke to you?'
the ruthless ringleader replies,
and the homeless man puts his hands up,
doing all he can to defend himself but
it's not enough, because despite his guarantees
he's now taking **blow after blow**:
fists, feet, knees.

They're all pounding away at him now
in a pack, relentless and non-stop like they're
Tyson Fury, Conor McGregor,
Oleksandr Usyk and KSI.
The longer it carries on,
with every passing second, the likelier
it is that this man could die.

The ordeal lasts half a minute or so
until one of the group –
familiar trainers,
recognizable body shape,
about my height,
one gloved hand –
bravely stands
in front of the man
to stop him taking any more blows
and begs, 'Allow it, boys,
I think he's had enough.'

Even from here, it's clear. It's Malachi.
He's wearing a black Blakely T-shirt
and a black Blakely cap.

I haven't really chatted to him since
before I went to Arvon.
I've not even seen him much
around school lately,
but I did get that text from him,
apologizing, around the time
we were looking for Maher,
but I was too busy at the time to reply,
which thinking about it now,
is kind of rude, as he comes
to this poor man's rescue.

The group's leader,
the devil in Palm Angels,
smirks at Malachi with an evil grin,

and then starts nodding menacingly
and says, 'Ah, I see, so little Malachi
fancies himself as a hero today, does he?'

Then on the ringleader's wordless command,
well, it looks like at least,
the rest of the group suddenly
run off at speed
up Prince of Wales Road,
laughing like hyenas
before turning right towards All Bar One,
cheering like World Cup final footballers
who've just scored a last-minute winner.

'You all right, mate?' Malachi says,
crouching down to wipe the man's face,
which is covered in blood and dripping
on the pavement to form thick red puddles.

His nose looks all broken and bent,
several cuts on his already-chapped lips.
His eyes are glassy and his voice is raspy
as he tries to shout, **'You fucking dickheads!'**
to the group of young men who have
already long disappeared into the Norwich night.

And before we have time to duck or hide,
Malachi turns round
and spots Leigh and me,
but he doesn't say anything,
or ask us *What you looking at?* angrily.

Instead he just stares at us,
a little lost, a little blankly.

···||·|·||·||···

For months now, Mr Bruce
has been constantly
going on about how good my pieces are,
saying that apart
from this writer called Frank O'Hara
(who I've never even heard of before),
I'm his favourite poet.

At least once a week he asks me
whether I've written something new.
Sometimes it feels like he's an addict
and he desperately needs a new song
or some new poetry of mine
to get his next fix.

It was actually his idea for me
to write something for Mum's birthday,
which we're celebrating with
a little party later today.
After all she's been through in
the last year or so, I'm keen
to make an effort to try and make the day
as special for her as I can.
So I've written her this poem,
especially as she's been saying how she's
really proud of me ever
since I came back from Arvon.

I've even saved up some
money to buy her a cake
and one of them massive **Birthday** badges.

I hope she likes what I've done.
I've been trying to use some of the things
I learned at Arvon in my writing –
little features here and there to bring out
certain images a bit more in my work. But
I think the thing I've learned the most
is to just be more confident.

And I feel like I've got more to say now,
because life is so different from how it used be
living back in Hackney:

new school,
new friends,
new ends.

It's all change for Mum too –
she's even met someone new.
For a few weeks now she's been keen
for me to spend more time with Carl,
a man she met at work,
in his fifties I think, covered in tattoos.

He seems all right, not Mum's usual type –
for starters, he's white –
but I don't care who she picks really,
as long as he's kind to her and treats her right.

I know what it can be like
to be judged because of the colour of your skin –
followed by the security guard in JD
when they think you're not looking,
being made fun of or called names.
Even though people can be
out of order sometimes,
ever since what happened to Maz,
my mission is to treat everybody the same.

With Mr Bruce's help,
I've printed out my poem for Mum
and put it in her card.

PROUD OF ME

money was always tight / not really been abroad
or even flown on a plane / it was just job centres
and benefits and being cold at night / not much
for dinner / a cheap takeaway to share / a large
portion of chips / and *listen / Ronny, are you
listening / whatever happens don't let the bailiffs
in* / cash-in-hand jobs cos they can't hold you back
because of the colour of your skin / nah / you're
too headstrong for that / not afraid to manage
the silence with your chest / yes / you had to be
streetwise / work during the day / rest / then
on to your night shifts / cross through the park
at midnight to get the bus / nah / not from here
originally but now on to new streets and now we've
arrived / I just want to make you proud of me /

**Mum, I love you and I'm listening / all I want to do –
after all you been through – is make you proud of me**

The party has begun, there's soca music
blaring out of the speakers, there's rum punch
and lots of food on the table:
jerk chicken, jerk fish, macaroni and cheese,
roast potatoes, coleslaw, and rice and peas.

Every five minutes or so the door knocks
and someone else comes in and the house
is filled with more people, more noise.
Some people I know,
like Leigh and his family, obviously,
and a couple people who live on our street.
Lots of people I've never met before, but I'm
guessing people Mum works with.

I'm about to give Mum the card
when there's another knock on the door and
as I open it I'm surprised to see Kemi,
standing in the doorway in his Liverpool top,
clutching a big bunch of
white roses and a little bag
from The Perfume Shop.

'Ronny, long time no see!' he says,
as he thinks about giving me a spud but then
decides to go for the hug.
The embrace is short but special.
I've not seen Kemi since he

dropped us off here last summer,
but it's really good to see him again.

I've missed bantering him about Liverpool
and just generally chatting about life and stuff.
He seems his usual happy and smiley self
as he asks, 'Where is she, then?
The birthday girl?'
I'm nervous to say anything –
I'm not sure how much he knows
about Carl and how awkward it might be
for them to just meet each other randomly.

Then as Carl steps into the hallway behind me,
wearing an old-school Chelsea jersey
and having just cracked open
another bottle of Birra Morreti,
there's this sort of stand-off between the two
and I'm just stood there,
caught in the crossfire,
stuck in the middle in no man's land,
not really knowing what to say,
not really knowing what to do.

Now we're all awkwardly in the sitting room,
as Skillibeng's 'Crocodile Teeth' comes on.
The mood is tense because Kemi,
who's usually this calm, level-headed guy,
looks a little all over the place as he eyes up Carl,
who sits opposite,
just trying to act normal and smile,

casually taking regular sips
from his bottle of beer.

Eventually Carl, having been
stared at for most of the day,
looks towards Kemi and says,
'Is there a problem here, mate?'

Then, just about loud enough
over the music to be
heard by everyone in the sitting room,
Kemi suddenly mumbles, 'Outside,'
through gritted teeth,
and it feels like it's all about to kick off.

Carl, without saying a word,
follows Kemi.
Mum tries to grab his hand as he
gets up to leave
but he shrugs it off,
looks her in her face and says,
'It's fine, trust me,'
as he starts taking off his jumper even
before he's stepped through the back door.

Mum and I follow them into the garden
and watch, as Carl dumps his hoodie on the grass
and Kemi does the same.
They both stand facing each other
like they're cowboys from an old Western film.

And for a moment I feel
like maybe it's on me
to do something, to referee,
to respond to this awkward
tension in some way because I don't want
Mum to get stressed again and
make herself ill, especially on her birthday.

Then, still without saying anything
to each other, Carl grabs a plant pot
and Kemi grabs a garden chair,
but they don't use these as weapons,
as I think they might.
They instead plop them down proper purposefully
and, as they check the dimensions,
the length and width,
it suddenly
becomes clear what they're setting up.
It's a makeshift pitch
with two makeshift goals at either end
of our little back garden.

They kick ball for a bit:
side-foot, toe-punt, laces.
Then after ten minutes or so of a random
high-intensity kickabout, red versus blue,
these two grown men
stop
playing.

Finally, they start walking
towards each other,
both hands outstretched,
ready to shake,
but at the last minute they change their mind
and hug instead.

APRIL

When I get to school on Monday morning,
something feels strange, and
instead of being told to go to class,
everybody in Key Stage 4 is directed
into the hall for a special assembly,
ushered down the corridor by
stressed-looking teachers,
not giving too much away.

Everyone's proper confused.
Leigh's just as baffled as me.
Whatever the news is it must be
big to miss English,
one of those all-important
core subjects, of course.

No one really knows what's going on,
but there are rumours circulating already
in hushed tones by the well-known
school gossips:

– exams are to be cancelled
– ITV news are coming to interview some of us
– dreaded OFSTED
(the teachers have been scared about this for months).

As we all whisper and speculate,
spouting different theories as we take our seats,
in walks the head teacher, Mr Shaughnessy,
who looks downcast and unhappy
as he straightens his tie, and solemnly

climbs the steps on to the stage
and braces himself to address us
with whatever news he has in store.

'Good . . .' he begins,
stutters, stammers,
clears his throat and tries again.

'Good morning, Key Stage four.
What I am about to say won't be easy to hear,
so it's best I get straight to the point quickly,'
he adds, before looking up despairingly
and taking a deep breath.

'I am afraid to say
that a valued member of our
school community – Malachi,
a Year Eleven student in Ms Colney's
tutor group, who joined us from the
beginning of Year Seven and
recently started at a local PRU temporarily
as part of a managed move,
to help and support him with some of his
additional needs, shall we say –
was sadly taken from us on Saturday.

'It's fair to say Malachi was going through a
difficult time of late,
a rough patch of sorts, had a lot on his plate
at home and away from school.
But no matter

the issues he was facing and
some of the problems
he was working through,
he was still just a young man,
sixteen years of age with
his whole life ahead of him, just like you.

'He will be sorely missed.
His precious, precious life
was taken from us far too easily.'

In response to this last line
from Mr Shaughnessy,
there are some audible sobs from
a few rows behind me,
as a blonde Year Eleven girl,
who I've seen around,
rummages into her blazer pocket
and hands a tissue to a boy
with glasses whose face is all red
and eyes all puffy.

Even Leigh, not Malachi's
biggest fan, obviously, looks in bits and
on the brink of tears.

Since coming back from Arvon
a few weeks ago, and running from the feds
that time in Chapelfield Gardens, Malachi
had stopped bothering me.
In fact, until that night in town,

after the footy, I hadn't really
seen him around as much, actually.

'There is an ongoing investigation
to find out what exactly happened,'
Mr Shaughnessy continues,
'and you'll probably
hear lots of reports and different stories
on the news over the next few days.
I know this might be difficult
for many of you,
so we're making extra sessions available
with Ms Spooner, the school counsellor,
who has agreed to stay till six
if you want to talk . . . and, of course,
as always,
my door is open.

'We will be sending flowers to his family
from the whole school today,
so if you wish to sign it too,
then the card will be left at reception
until the end of the day.'

Leigh is fully crying now,
but I don't really know
what to think, to be honest.
I only knew Malachi a bit, and I am
shocked and sad too that his life
ended in this tragic way,
but I can't help thinking about Maz right now,

reminded of the day
he was stabbed to death
in London, last May.

I can't help but *feel*
that no matter where you are,
no matter what part of the country you live in,
being a young boy, sometimes
in the **wrong place**
at the **wrong time**
through the **wrong eyes**,
can be **deadly**.

ıııı||ıı||ıııı

It can be mad confusing
being a teenager sometimes,
made even harder by others in school,
if you don't tread careful.

It's like a melting pot of emotions
and different identities,
changing constantly,
swirling around and around,
up and down.
One day you can feel the **darkest lows**,
the next, the **highest highs**;
you can go from being
an outsider and uncool
to being much loved
in a matter of months.

Popularity is fickle, so dependent
on who can afford to wear the right clothes
and the right trainers,
behave a certain way day to day,
post the right thing at the right time online,
have something really interesting to say;
likes, followers, subscribers:
numbers, numbers, numbers.

When I joined back in September,
the other students seemed
not to want to know me,
constantly eyeing me up and down suspiciously,
unable to work me out,
not interested in finding out what I'm all about.

Now I have a pretty large circle of friends,
including, at the top of the list, Leigh, of course,
who is not as chatty in class as he was before –
not since Arvon and meeting Charlie –
and his mock grades are starting to improve
because of it too.

He's a new person, to be honest.

Without being boastful,
bigging myself up too much,
now it seems
everyone wants to hang out with me
in some capacity, unlike before;
in the last few months or so

you could say there's been a real shift –
it's all been a bit weird, actually.

The big thing everyone keeps telling me
is that I should apply to be Head Boy
next year.

At the end of every lesson, more or less,
every teacher has been keeping me behind,
and not because I've got a detention
but to have a little chat and suggest that I should
go for the role, put my application form in,
give it a go.
But I just don't know.
I'm not sure if I'll be any good –
I've not even been here that long.

Long enough, though, to know
that there are a few problems
that need addressing:
like the Year Elevens addicted to vaping
and the Year Eight boys who think they're
old-school shotters,
selling sweets in the toilets
like it's some illegal Class A and
they're experienced drug dealers,
unaware that it's foolishness like that,
that they're trying to replicate
in their own immature way,
that probably got Malachi
killed last Saturday.

Newspapers have been saying there's been
a rise of county lines in Norwich
in the last few years;
I hope it doesn't get so bad
that Mum thinks we should move again.
Not now, not just as I'm
starting to really like it here,
not just as I'm starting to make my mark.

We don't even have many
sessions with Lucas left,
which is kinda sad really,
as I can't believe
I've enjoyed his sessions
as much as I have.

Lucas's overexcitement,
his ankle-swinging trousers,
his brightly coloured socks,
and thick-soled Dr. Martens.
His whole vibe.

In so many ways, because of him,
I've learned that I have permission
to write whatever I want to write,
however I want to write it
in the classroom, but also
outside it too.

How the tables have turned, literally.
Leigh and I have gone from sitting at the

very back, excluding ourselves from
the rest of the class,
not overly keen to get involved . . .
to choosing to sit at the very front,
within touching distance of Lucas.
Not quite teacher's pet,
more like *Poet's Pet*, you could say.

'So, Year Ten,' he belts out
with a big booming voice
to ensure he has everyone's attention
in a semi-stern, semi-friendly way.
'Firstly, good to see you all.
I know I say this every time
but coming here and working with you is
the highlight of my Friday –
actually, my whole week.

'As usual, to start,
our Five-minute Free-write,
but there'll be no props today –
my bank balance simply can't take it . . .'
he exclaims overdramatically.

'Luckily, though, I bought these
a while back,' he adds as he
delves into his tote bag –
a new blue and orange one
that says **Burley Fisher Books** on it –
and emerges with a fistful of soft colourful dice.

'So, guys, today
we're going to try something new.
These are Story Starter Cubes
and they can be used
to work out the **What, Where, Who?**
of your poem.'

Lucas gives Leigh
the first dice to roll like he's
delivering a special invitation.
It's the blue one, the **who?**

Leigh cups the squidgy
cube in both hands and
begins to shake it vigorously,
like he's got a cocktail shaker
and he's a barman from a bougie bar in the city.
He eventually rolls it with
a little too much force, though,
so it bobbles off the table
and off other students' shoes,
before coming to a gradual stop
on the other side of the drama studio,
too far for either me or Leigh to see
what it says.

'It says . . . **boy**!'
Evelyn shouts from a few tables along.

Lucas hands me the red one to roll,
which I do much more cautiously than Leigh.
It reads: **calls the police**.

Dylan rolls the yellow:
in the city.

'So, pretty self-explanatory from here really.
I want you to draft something loosely
related to the prompt:
A boy – calls the police – in the city.
All clear? Good.' Lucas says, before anyone
has the time to question or query.
'Your five minutes start . . . *ed* ten seconds ago,
so hurry up; come on, off you go!'

Responding to the challenge,
my thoughts immediately
turn to Maz and then to Malachi
and what might have been
if either of them managed to ring the police
before what happened to them . . . happened.

No one really knows what exactly
went down with Malachi still –
the police investigation remains ongoing –
but despite what some people
might have thought of him,
the rumour going round is that
it could actually be
a(nother) case of mistaken identity.

As Lucas's timer ticks down,
I pour all my emotion on to the page
and write straight from the heart.

Handwriting doesn't matter,
neither do spelling or grammar.

I'm not sure what it is; it's not
quite a poem or a short story.
It's longer than just a list,
it's not a song, essay or rant.
It's just words, that's what I keep telling myself.
It's just words, so I just keep writing
one
word
after
another.

After the five minutes are up, like always now,
I've written a lot, like ten, eleven lines, and
even though my wrist feels a bit stiff
and my heart is all tender and sore,
doing that Five-minute Free-write
has made me feel better than I did before.

I don't feel like reading out what I've written
for now. Just feels a little too personal
and still a bit too rough, but
lots of the class do and it's always
cool to see what they've come up with.

'Now, for our main writing exercise today,'
Lucas explains, 'we're going to look at a
special form of poem,
one that goes back centuries –

well, I imagine so anyway –
called an ode.

'Through the years, poets have written
odes literally about all sorts of things,
so let's start by looking at
this one by Raymond Antrobus,
someone I know rather well actually,'
Lucas says in a semi-smug kind of way.
'He's written "Ode to My Hair".

'Ray is a poet of mixed heritage,
so his hair doesn't always
fit the mould, shall we say;
sometimes makes him stand out,
especially when he goes to see his
Jamaican family, who occasionally
make comments about its texture, *et cetera*.
So, unlike some other odes,
his isn't all lovely and gushing,
but actually his relationship with the subject
is a little more tricky.

'Your ode could be about anything at all:
your pet, a body part, your favourite food,
where you like to hang out on weekends,
or a YouTuber like Mr Beast, Sidemen or Speed.
Literally about anything or anybody.

'You have fifteen minutes to see
what you can come up with.

'You might choose to write in
the second person – **you** –
but as always I will leave that creative decision
entirely up to **you**.

'Your time starts . . . **Now!**'

I have a few ideas that I'm playing with
to write about, possibly:

an ode to **Maz**
an ode to **Malachi**
an ode to **Lana**.

Maybe even a piece
that combines all three,
and is about being
a young person generally.

Or maybe something about football,
and still being a fan of the
so-called *beautiful game*
but more and more in a different way
than just playing it these days.

It's difficult though; I'm not quite sure,
so instead I decide to continue working
on something from before,
a song of sorts.

After the fifteen minutes are up
I've written something, not really
a response to the ode activity,
but more of a piece I've called
'Stuck in the Mud'.
I let Leigh read
a bit from my notebook and he gives me
an approving nod as if to say,
This is special, Ronny,
really special.

MAY

No one knows,
not Mum or any teacher,
but Leigh and I have decided
not to go to school today.

I haven't missed
a single day all year but
there is somewhere
more important to be.

Today, even though we have:
double Maths,
double English
and double PE,
today, we're going to a funeral –
Malachi's.

I put my uniform on like normal,
made sure Mum saw me dressed
and ready before she left for work,
knowing it was key to keep the act up:
shirt, school tie,
trousers and jumper.

To be honest
I don't like lying, or missing lessons,
but going in today
just felt like the wrong thing to do.

It's all been planned properly.
We printed out fake letters –

I'm apparently seeing a physio
in London for an old football injury,
and Leigh's apparently at the university
graduation of his older brother in Leeds
(which was actually last week).

I didn't even know Malachi
that long, or even that deeply,
but I can't help but feel somehow
like what happened to him
could have happened to me.
I was just seconds away from being sucked
in that time in Chapelfields,
tempted into doing
something that I shouldn't
but could have done easily.

Leigh and I agree to meet
on Unthank Road, by Caffè Nero,
and then make our way round
the corner to the church.
We're not planning on actually
speaking to his friends and family
but just take it all in from somewhere
close enough to pay our respects
in our own little way.

Leigh arrives soon after me and
he's dressed in a black suit,
shiny black tie and
gem-studded
red-bottomed loafers.

Even though Leigh is usually
in good spirits, always happy-go-lucky,
there's something noticeably
downhearted about his mood today,
clearly affected by what's happened,
which is understandable really.

We head towards Holy Trinity Church,
standing just round the corner
from the entrance,
arriving in time to see
the hearse as it turns at
the bottom of the road
and creeps closer,
super slowly.

Two men walk in front,
dressed all smart,
clutching their posh-looking hats
as a mark of respect.

There's a wreath with yellow
and green flowers inside the hearse,
the colours of Norwich City,
resting on the oak-brown coffin
with shiny brass handles.
The flowers spell out **MALACHI**
on one side of the window,
and **SON**, I think, on the other.
There are football scarves
draped over the polished box.

Even normal people –
just out walking their dog
or buying a newspaper
or going to the post office –
stop to pay their respects.
Like the old man lugging his shopping trolley,
wearing those shoes
with one big Velcro strap,
who takes off his hat,
and looks at the slow-moving
church-bound vehicle like
there's an old friend inside,
a fellow war veteran or something.

Leigh and me continue watching from
a short distance away
a little further down the road,
half-crouching in between
a white Ford Focus
and a little silver Peugeot,
not wanting to be spotted
and told to go back to school.

We watch the mourners
clamber out of the cars
and gather on the gravel and the grass
outside the church.
Hands either buried deep
into their pockets,
or scrunching up tissues
used to dab swollen eyes.

Then, slowly emerging from one
of the long black cars
following the hearse,
we see Malachi's family:
dressed in their Sunday best
and wearing little bits of jewellery,
necklaces and rings and things.

His mum's being consoled by
friends and family:
hugged tight, shoulder rubbed, and kissed.
Little acts of kindness
to try and make her feel better,
but his dad's struggling to keep it all in,
head bowed, sinking
lower
and **lower**
with the weight of the grief.

Just as the family start shuffling their way
into the church
for the start of the service,
this tinted-windowed Range Rover Sport
suddenly screams down the road,
drill music blaring,
piercing the peace like a machete.
It's a song that sounds like
Rimzee's 'Entrepreneur'
the nearer it gets.

The car skids to a stop
and almost at the same time
this group of men, five of them,
all in their late teens,
early twenties possibly, climb out and
start dusting themselves down.

They all look familiar, even from afar.

They're dressed smart, but in a casual way:
black suits, dangling silver chains.
Black turtlenecks.
Black Air Forces.
Black Ray-Bans.

Some of them have flowers,
big expensive-looking bunches.

I definitely recognize two of the younger ones
from that night at Chapelfield Gardens:
the boy that was eating the Cheetos
and the other one
that was doing Mo Gilligan impressions.

The driver comes out last
and I recognize him immediately as
the leader of the group from before,
the one that was kicking and punching
the homeless man outside Tesco;
the boss, the top boy, the one
who calls the shots, probably.

He wears a loud lilac suit
with matching tasselled loafers.

Even from our place of safety
hiding across the other side of the street,
their presence is still making me feel
a little uneasy.

From here, I can see
that the mother's face is
a combination of sadness,
fire and **fury**.
She's far from happy at seeing
the arrival of this ***good-for-nothing gang***.

A man – Malachi's dad, or stepdad maybe –
is trying to hold her back, grabbing her
by both shoulders and using all his force
to stop her lunging at them.

The leader in the lilac suit
stands unmoved at first, not sure
whether to react or just leave it.
Even from here you can see he's
contemplating his options
lingering in limbo.
But soon enough he
gets proper agitated and angry,
and seconds later he snaps,
and starts cussing
before chucking

the bunch of flowers
he brought at her feet disgustedly.

He then yanks his turtleneck up
and starts pointing at something
strapped to his waist, causing
the crowd of mourners
to gasp and begin
slowly
backing
away.

Everyone except for Malachi's mum,
who doesn't show a flicker of fear
but looks even more furious than before
as this guy waves something about:
something **sharp**,
or something **loaded** –
from here, it's unclear.

'You see that, yeah, you see that?'
The guy is yelling and I can tell
Leigh's itching to help
and I sort of want to as well,
but as I watch the madness
unfold in front of my eyes I'm stuck,
completely rooted to the spot
frozen with fear,
rigid with shock,
barely able to look,
desperate to hide, desperate to run,

suddenly feeling a little lightheaded,
jelly-legged and weak.
Images of **Maz**,
images of **Malachi**
making me feel proper unsteady
on my feet.

'Come, man, just leave it!'
one of the other boys says
loud enough for us to hear,
grabbing the arms of the big boss
in the lilac-coloured suit
and ushering him back to the Range Rover.

The rest get into the car quickly
as if keen to get away
from a crime scene suddenly,
and within seconds they speed past us,
up the road and out of sight,
music blaring even louder than
when they first arrived.

'You OK, Ron?' Leigh asks
as I take a deep breath
to try and feel normal
and grounded again.
While back outside the church,
Malachi's mum is on her knees
now, sobbing and wailing,
bent in on herself on all fours on the ground,
and one of the first people on hand

to rush to her side
and provide some extra support
is our head teacher,
Mr Shaughnessy.

᎐᎐᎐||᎐|᎐||᎐᎐᎐

Friday morning, back to usual settings.
Twenty-two students.
Drama studio.
Me and Leigh sat in the front seats,
intrigued to know what madness Lucas
has come up with this week.

This is our last session before we
type up our pieces for the class anthology,
and my desire to write stories
burns brighter than ever:

memories about Maz,
lines about Lana,
lyrics about Malachi.

We did a little starter free-write where we
listened to this pretty cool French rap song
called 'Rufio' by La F and
wrote down any English words that
came to mind as we took in
the sounds of the track.

While listening, I picked out words like:
studio, **sirens**, **smoke**, **power** and **money**
first time round and
then we started writing
while the song played again.

Next, Lucas handed out a wordsearch
and instructed us to jot down
the first ten words we found
and use them to write something new
in five minutes.

E	L	H	E	L	Y	C	F	L	O	W	W	L	S
P	I	D	B	M	H	R	W	I	R	I	Y	T	L
S	O	F	M	U	S	I	C	A	L	L	A	R	R
T	O	E	T	T	E	C	E	H	T	D	M	T	H
A	O	E	T	S	T	K	A	S	W	T	T	L	Y
D	O	A	T	R	L	E	M	B	T	H	L	D	T
I	A	S	L	U	Y	T	R	D	T	A	W	Y	H
U	M	T	C	I	S	Y	D	H	B	Y	I	T	M
M	I	M	A	G	E	L	P	T	Y	M	M	I	A
P	P	E	L	C	M	T	O	S	I	M	C	T	O
I	A	I	R	E	C	O	S	K	T	L	E	N	E
O	C	C	T	T	F	A	T	Y	T	E	Y	E	L
R	D	E	E	W	M	P	I	W	I	I	W	D	D
S	T	T	W	L	E	N	I	R	D	A	E	I	K

It was actually a pretty cool activity to do,
and I liked the little piece I came up with too.

'Now, time for a surprise,' Lucas says,
'literally!' weaving in between
the tables and handing out
from a different little black tote
that reads **NATIONAL CENTRE FOR WRITING**
actual Kinder Surprise chocolate eggs.

Even though we're all in Year Ten,
fourteen, fifteen years old,
it's hard to contain our genuine excitement
as we pick off the foil wrapper
and prise open the
golden egg to see what's inside.

Lucas tells us to
write a poem about whatever
our toy is, but make it seem
even more formidable than it
appears on the surface.

My 'surprise' is a little plastic rabbit,
muscular with pointed ears, on a green base.
I write down a title,
the first words I can think of:
'The Hench Rabbit', I call it for now,
prompting Leigh to
look over my shoulder and say,
'That's a hare, you know, by the way.'

'Whatever, man – rabbit, hare,
I don't care,' I reply
semi-defensively, as I scribble
a few words on to my page.

It's another predictably wacky Lucas task,
but one that has us all writing again.
Everyone, that is, except for Leigh,
who, just as I'm getting into
the swing of it,
nudges my shoulder
and looks all serious at me.

'So . . . speaking of surprises,' he starts,
'I suppose this is a good time
to share some news.'
He's fiddling with his little toy,
thumbing the face of a plastic kangaroo
nervously.

'This sounds really deep
but I'm telling you because you're such a
kind-hearted and open-minded person, Ronny,'
he adds, clearly struggling
to find the right words
for whatever it is he wants to say.

'Right now, I'm in the process of
finding myself in this stupidly
"Top G"-obsessed world we live in,
finding the real me and embracing a new,
previously mistaken identity.

'I'm not just a boy, Ronny.
That label just don't fit my personality
I've come to realize recently.
So from today I'm changing
my pronouns to **they/them**
as I begin the transition to
becoming non-binary.'

It's quite a shock and I look at them to see
how serious they're being.
Leigh's the class clown at the best of times,
but after reading the frankness of their face,
holding their gaze
for a wordless moment or two,
I give them the **tightest hug I can**.

'Oh and by the way,
another surprise of sorts, you could say,
I know you're applying to be
Head Boy and, Ronny, believe me,
I *really* want you to get it, obviously,'
they say, clutching my hand tightly.
'But I hope it's OK that I'm thinking of
applying for the role too,
not because I want to compete with you,
but I'd be doing it for the new me,
if you get what I mean.'

I look up towards the ceiling,
screw up my face a little in fake fury
and then return their fixed stare.

'I do, I really do,' I tell them.
'You're basically no better than a sheep –
anything I want to do,
you have to do it too,'
I say with a semi-stern
expression that slowly
turns into a playful grin,
clearly joking,
as I give them another **long hug**.

JUNE

'**Final question of the Norwich round,'**
Carl, the quizmaster tonight, says over the mic.
'**What phrase would you find**
under the Welcome to Norwich sign,
seen as you enter the centre of the city?'

My brain starts to ache a bit
because I know that I know this.
But *damn, what is it again?*
I definitely remember seeing it
the day we moved here.

Leigh isn't really helping and
is casually filing their nails,
more interested in how they look
than coming up with
suggestions to the question
they would probably know the answer to,
if they were actually listening.

In hindsight, they're
probably not the best
team-mate to have tonight.
They're not dumb or anything like that,
but let's just say, they have
different priorities.

I look around and everyone else
is scribbling away
in their little groups, clearly confident
with the answer they've just put.

On the *Trust Us, We're Teachers* table:
Mr Bruce, Mr Shaughnessy,
Mrs Stratton and Mrs Barnham-Broom
are looking pleased,
but on the big table in the corner
of this little pub, The Rose Tavern,
Malachi's family –
his mum, stepdad,
uncle and aunty,
simply called *Team Malachi* – are
knocking spirits down to try
and keep spirits up,
still looking sad,
despite their best attempts
to put on a brave face.

Our team, which we've called
Where's My Bum Bum Cream?
(just because we thought it sounded funny),
is made up of Mum, Lucas the poet
and his wife, Molly, me and Leigh.

I just can't remember the answer;
Mum doesn't have a clue,
Leigh's still not helping either,
Lucas says it's on the tip of his tongue
and before I have time to at least
have a guess . . .

'OK! It's time to
swap your answer sheet,' Carl says.

'We'll go through the answers
to this round in just a minute or two –'

'But before you do,' Mum interrupts,
raising her voice a little,
before rising from her seat gingerly,
one hand on her belly,
shuffling her way to the front
to take the mic from Carl.

'G . . . good evening . . .' she starts,
causing everyone, including me,
to cover both their ears immediately,
as the microphone starts whining
really loudly.

As quickly as he can,
Carl fiddles with a knob on the speaker
to try and stop the feedback
from deafening everyone.

'Good evening, all,'
Mum tries again,
this time much more quietly.

'Just another reminder as to why
we're all here tonight,' she says.
'A young man we all knew, and who
was loved by many – Malachi –
was taken from us
less than a couple of miles from here.'

Mum points in a direction
beyond the far corner of the pub.
'And, as a community, we
must come together to make sure
this doesn't happen to our
young men again.'

There's a collective nod of agreement
from everyone in the pub basically.

'We're grateful to have
Malachi's family with us tonight,
at this difficult time,' Mum says,
looking towards the table to the right.

'Remember, your quiz entry fee,
your donations, the food and drink
bought at the bar,
the raffle ticket to hopefully
win one of many amazing prizes –
including a whole crate of Prime
from the team at Lincoln Shopper –
it's all for a good cause.
All the proceeds, every single penny,
will go to the Go Wild Golden Triangle
Youth Group, who offer trips,
food parcels for families,
and a space for young boys and girls
to make friends, have a free after-school snack,
play games, sport and most importantly,'
she says, clutching the mic tight

with both her hands, 'to stay safe
from the hands of drug-dealing gangs.'

As she stands there,
clearly a bit nervous and shy,
I think she's done amazingly
to set all this up at short notice
and bring everyone together like this:

– got Carl to write a quiz
– found a venue
– invited many of the teachers from school
– got Malachi's family to come too
– brought together the wider Norwich community.

All here
in memory of Malachi.

As she heads back to her seat,
a ripple of applause gets
louder and **louder** and **louder**
till literally everyone is on their feet.

When the clapping eventually stops,
Carl taps the mic and says,
'OK – time to swap
your answer sheets.'
Reminding everyone that there's a quiz still on.

I use the break to go for a piss,
choosing the privacy

of the only cubicle over using the urinal,
when a voice that's unmistakably Leigh's,
shouts, but in a
hushed-whisper sort of way,
'Hurry up in there, Shakespeare!
I've got something for you!'

'I'm kinda busy,' I shout back,
but also wonder what it might be
that Leigh is so desperate to show me.

As I finish up, unlock the door
and pull it open, Leigh charges in
straightaway so that we're both
now in this tiny space,
and locks it back up immediately
behind them.

From an inside pocket
of their leather jacket
they pull out little bottles of
red-lidded Magnum tonic wine
that say 16.5% ALCOHOL on the label.

It's definitely one of those drinks I've seen
uncles and aunties clutching
at family barbecues and weddings
in London, back in the day,
being gripped and sipped
morning, afternoon and
long into the night.

TONIC WINE   WINE

God knows where they
got the Maggies from
and how they've managed to find
what is typically a drink drunk
within the Black community
here in Norwich, but they're clearly
very pleased with themselves.

'It's lethal, Ronny, I'm telling you,'
they say with a glint in their eye.
'Managed to get two each,'
as they hand me the bottles
and I tentatively untwist the top.

'A toast,' Leigh says,
raising the cap aloft,
'to Malachi.'

'To Malachi,' I respond,
as we clink our lids and
take our first sips.

'To Maz too,' I then add,
as I down the rest of the shot,
which actually doesn't taste *that* bad.

We head back to the quiz and
the round is *science and nature* now,
not something I know much about,
but all the questions tonight
link to stuff that Malachi liked,

including ones about animals,
which makes sense after seeing how
he interacted with the little muntjac
that time in the exam hall.

And as the quiz goes on,
through the different rounds:
entertainment, *general knowledge*
and one about *Norwich City*,
Leigh and I continue to take
regular secret trips to the toilet
for regular secret sips of Maggie,
and I soon start to feel fully pissed,
all gassed and giddy,
the words from the quiz questions
not really going in.

We're now polishing off
our second bottles and
I'm starting to feel proper funny,
all woozy and dizzy.

No doubt about it,
we're drunk.
Drunk
drunk.

DRUUUUUUUUNK.

And after ten or fifteen more minutes,
I start to actually feel a bit sick,

an ache that started at the pit
of my stomach rising higher and higher,
lingering in my throat,
and in the middle of the quiz
covering my mouth with a hand,
I sprint to the loo as fast as I can,
hoping I make it to the toilet in time.

As I slump over the bowl,
I feel a soothing hand on my back.

'Oh, Ronny, this is not how big brothers
should behave, is it?' Mum asks,
(I think)
as she plucks out some fluff from my Afro.

For many reasons
I can't make sense of
right now . . .
I have no idea what she's talking about.

'I'm pregnant, Ronny –
me and Carl are having a baby.'

I'm just about to speak,
say something to show my shock,
feeling somewhere between *That's amazing, Mum*
and *What the actual fuck?*, when
I sense a thickness rise up my throat
and, too late to stop it now,
gush out **thunderously**
into the toilet bowl.

I think about Leigh . . .
(Do they feel as rough as me?)

I picture Lana . . .
(I'm kind of glad she's not here to see me like this.)

I think about the fact I'm about to become a big brother . . .
(Wtf!)

But through the fogginess of my thoughts,
one rises up above all the others.

'I remember it now, Mum.

'**A FINE CITY** . . . that's what it says
on the WELCOME TO NORWICH sign . . .

'a fi–' I start to say one more time,
before vomiting up even more tonic wine.

JULY

I take a **deep breath**.

Comb out my ever-growing Afro,
make sure I look my best,
and then clear my throat and
stroll in confidently, carefully
clutching a big blown-up picture that
I've got with me.

'Good morning, Ronny,
please do take a seat,'
says a tired-looking Mr Shaughnessy,
who's definitely not been
the same energetic figure
he was since the death of Malachi.

The set-up is all really official and formal with
Mr Shaughnessy, the current Head Boy
and Head Girl sat behind the table
alongside Mrs Barnham-Broom, the deputy,
with their notebooks and pens at the ready.

'All set?' Sir asks, and I nod, a bit shyly.
'So, Ronny, to begin, in your own words,
why do you wish to be
Head Boy next year?'

'No offence, Sir, and I hope
you don't take this the wrong way,' I say,
'but I'd like to
answer your question, in fact, conduct

this whole interview,
in my own special way.

'Essentially, Sir, ever since my
incredible week at Arvon
I've been working on this new song
called **"Stuck in the Mud"**,'
as I turn the canvas round and reveal the
photo that Leigh took of me
in Eaton Park the other week.

Mr Shaughnessy studies the image and
pretends to look excited but kind
of looks more confused about where
I'm going with it.

In fact, all the panel's faces look a little puzzled.
My reply to their first question is unconventional.
But I plough on fearlessly and
connect my phone to my Bluetooth speaker
to play a Harvey Gunn instrumental.

I take a deep breath,
recite the first few words
from the first line in my head.

I grew up in a place that like mud could be sticky . . .

and then wait for the beat to drop
before I properly begin.

'This is an original piece,' I say,
'all about me, basically,
to help you understand my life,
where I come from and the
beginnings of my story . . .'

STUCK IN THE MUD

**I grew up in a place that like mud could be sticky
where we feared the police and not necessarily
because we'd done wrong, but mainly**

because in their eyes we
look a certain way
that didn't conform
to their idea of the norm
or act in a way that to them was not OK

I clear my throat a little and start the next bit . . .

My time away has taught me
that I should be Black and proud
and I shouldn't be embarrassed to be
who I am or where I come from
Yes, my Mum received benefits
but she used it as a springboard
so now deserves universe-al credit
for keeping us safe and fed
and safe from harm, safe from the feds

The ends can be a battlefield
I've seen friends dead for stupidness
taken away from me dramatically
just for having the boldness to be

I grew up in a place that like mud could be sticky . . .

Now on to the chorus . . .

Cos we're trying out here, we're all going through stuff
cos we're dying out here, all we need is a little love
stuck in the mud these times, it's time we got unstuck
stuck in the mud these times, it's time we wipe it off

I'm feeling OK as I start the next verse,
and for a moment, just a split second or two,
I close my eyes and allow myself to imagine
I'm not in a secondary school
in Norfolk, but instead,
right here, right now,
for a brief moment
I'm performing in front of thousands
of adoring fans on the main stage at Glastonbury.

I get emotional sometimes
like that programme Repair Shop
writing and writing lines,
just waiting for the beat to drop.
want to make more money than the Pointless jackpot
writing line after line
the hustle with my pen will never stop
Pen in one hand, on my wrist, a ticking clock
I've got to make this work, just need a little luck
Young boys who look like me dying on our streets,
when will enough be enough?
Life isn't fair as a boy from the ends,
when will people wake up?

As I repeat the chorus, I have a
little glimpse at the faces of the panel,
but they're still not giving much away.

Not a fan of mince pies, just humble ones
without this love I feel, I'd be just a homeless bum
Hope for a helping hand and better days to come
even unlucky number 13 has to be lucky for some

> So walk with me on this path in the spring sun
> and get annoyed with me when our kreps get caked in mud
> Get lost, cold and tired, let's find a stick to scrape it off
> One hug from you will make these tough times less tough

On to the bridge.

> Emotional times, this is gonna be a hard one, still,
> but believe me when I say that my hustle is real
> and my love for this life will always shine,
> writer's block sometimes but just
> gotta keep my head up high,
> cos I still made it through
> months gone by,
> people asking me how and why?
> Told them I'm still writing lines, giving it my best try

Then the chorus again to end.

> cos we're trying out here, we're all stuck in some mud
> cos we're dying out here, we all need a little love
> stuck in the mud these times, it's time we got unstuck
> stuck in the mud these times, it's time we wipe it off

I turn off the Bluetooth speaker before
it automatically starts to play
the next song, and return to my seat
in front of the panel of four.

I actually don't know if I've nailed it or not.
I think I've probably performed it better

in front of the mirror at home but I don't
think it went terribly either,
but it's hard to tell.

I hope my song has covered all the bases,
shown these blank faces
that I've got what it takes
to be a good role model and more.

I incorporated little gestures here and there,
like Louise taught me at Arvon,
to help remember the words.
I stumbled a little in the middle,
but I carried on, tried to not
let the disappointment
of messing up show on my face and ruin
the rest of the performance.

But the expressions of the panel of four
sat in front of me are hard to read – perhaps
they are a little unsure,
too taken aback
with what I've just done,
it's hard to say.
None of them are giving much away.

I feel the need to say something more,
clarify where I was coming from.
'Basically, Sir, I chose to reply this way because
someone was telling me
the other day about this uni student from UEA.

I think he was doing an English degree and
instead of doing a proper formal essay he
submitted music as his final year
dissertation piece, and
ended up getting the top mark.'

Mr Shaughnessy nibbles the end
of his Bic pen as he listens carefully.

'I looked it up when I got home
and it was all true,
and I'm not gonna lie,
it really inspired me to
try something a little different today too.'

'Well, thanks for that very
interesting response, Ronny,'
says Mr Shaughnessy.
'This is my fifth year here
conducting these interviews and I'm not sure
I've heard anything quite like that before . . .

'What about you, Mrs Barnham-Broom?
Any initial thoughts, anything to say?'

She **pauses**, **hesitates** and **deliberates**,
begins to add something and then refrains.

'Well, it certainly was original!'
says the current Head Girl,
not really knowing what else to say,

looking down at her notes
and then looking away.

Clearly I've blown it.

ılı|ılı|ıılı

When I got home Mum was hounding me
every second to find out how I got on,
saying that she'd made mac and cheese
and spicy peri peri chicken especially
to celebrate, but deep down I just
couldn't predict the outcome
and had no inkling at all whether I'd done
enough to convince them.

'Don't get too stressed, Ronny,'
Mum says. 'You should be proud of
yourself, whatever happens,
for everything you've achieved this year.'

Despite her reassuring words,
the wait to find out was still kind of tense.
It seemed that I cared about getting the role
more than I thought I did.

Then at lunchtime
two whole days later,
I was instructed to go to
Mr Shaughnessy's office,
told by my tutor, Ms Stratton,
that finally a decision had been made.

I followed Sir into his office tentatively
and as he offered me a seat,
I saw that he was halfway through reading
Matt Haig's *The Midnight Library*.
I spotted too, a framed picture of his family –
his wife and two
young boys on holiday
somewhere sunny and sandy
like Dubai, or somewhere in Spain maybe.

This was the first time I'd been in here.
There was a little sofa in the corner
and a mounted LG TV screen that showed
school-related events on loop:
GCSE timetables, prom information
for the Year Elevens and
a list of all the after-school clubs.

He hung his navy blue blazer
with purple paisley lining
on the back of his chair and
sat directly opposite me,
rolled up his sleeves and
clasped his hands together.

'Ronny, I know it wasn't easy
here at first,' he said.
'East Anglia is very different from East London,
even more so for a person of colour, I'm sure.

'I grew up in a place called Dagenham
originally, Ronny, which sort of

sits on the outskirts of Essex,
not a million miles away
from Hackney.

'Was raised by my loving
but very strict Irish parents.
Was the first in my family to go to university,
even used to play centre-back
for the local football team,
Dagenham and Redbridge . . . well,
before they were called that.
It was just Dagenham back then;
now they play in the National League.

'I know it's not always easy to be
constantly high-achieving,
coming from the places we have,' he said.
'It can feel like we
always have something to prove
and that can be . . . exhausting,
to say the least, shall I say,'
he added with a sigh,
heavily reddened eyes
and bags bulging to the brim.
'But we deserve our seat at the table too.
Trust me, Ronny, you do,' he said despondently,
staring at the back wall behind me and
then high up at the ceiling, as if wanting to
communicate something to Malachi.

'Anyway,' he then said, snapping
out of some kind of daze,

'I expect you're itching to know
the outcome of your rather
unique interview?'

He slowly rose from his seat.
'Essentially, the fact of the matter is,
despite my little digression,
I think congratulations
are in order,' he said,
as he extended his hand for me to shake
with a big smile on his face.
'Very well done, Ronny,
you should be very, very proud.'

I'd done it!

From being an outsider from London,
a Black boy who some assumed was trouble,
to this, to now, here, Head Boy.

And ever since the news,
Mum (and Carl too actually),
has been acting crazy pleased,
taking every opportunity to kiss and hug me.

Even though she's now a few months' pregnant,
Mum's been dancing around the
living room and jumping on the settee,
telling everyone she knows basically –
all the residents at the care home where she works,
and all her cleaning friends – about me
and how proud she is of my journey.

I even got a **CONGRATULATIONS!** card from Kemi,
with the Liverpool player Mo Salah
on the front, just to annoy me.
But it's cool. I let him off
because inside the card
was also some money.

Since the announcement,
I've already been asked to
perform at the Year Eleven prom
at Park Farm Hotel next week,
and again at the Lord Mayor's Parade
next month with Leigh,
as Miss De La Mare, accompanying me
as a support act, of sorts.

Mr Shaughnessy has even asked me to be
the school's brand-new Poet Laureate,
a role that involves
writing original pieces about school events
for the termly newsletter,
but also performing in special assemblies and
teaching my own writing workshops
to Key Stage 3 groups.

But the biggest news was that Leigh
was also chosen to be
a 'Head Person', so that this year,
unlike before, there would be three 'Head People':
Me, Evie and Leigh,
who identify as

boy,
girl and
non-binary,
respectively.

It's just been mad ever since.
The other day we even got the chance to show
a reporter and photographer
from the local Norwich paper around.

I took them to the new display
by the main staircase
in the new block,
something I'm quite proud of because
there's a couple of lines taken from
'Stuck in the Mud'
that've been blown up.

They've put the school's logo in the corner
and framed it so everyone
from all years can clearly see.
I think it looks the business, actually.

Stuck in the mud, it's time we got unstuck
Stuck in the mud, it's time we wipe it off

The picture they took for the article is of us three
(and Mr Shaughnessy) standing in front of the display.
It was put on the school website
and Mr Shaughnessy said that he was also going to add it
to the school prospectus and end-of-year newsletter.

In the picture, we're all looking proper happy,
smiling so widely, clearly
pleased to be wearing
our new special **HEAD PEOPLE** ties,
which I'm so proud of,
I hang it up on the handle
of my wardrobe in my bedroom
like it's a World Cup winner's medal.

As it dangles there at night,
it's concrete evidence that I'm
one
step
closer
on this journey
to achieving my dreams.

The tie is basically the last thing I see
before I go to sleep.
Well, that and my iPhone screensaver of Lana,
who, even though we live like two,
three hours apart from each other,
has never been closer.

She easily lives in my head rent-free,
especially because she practically WhatsApps me
every night with the same message that leaves
me feeling all ecstatic and weak,
and reads:

> I'm so proud of you Ronny xxx

EPILOGUE

The departure board inside
Norwich Station says
the train for Cambridge leaves
in fourteen minutes,
which is just enough time for Leigh and me
to get mocha frappuccinos,
with whipped cream.

This afternoon, we're having a mini
Arvon reunion, of sorts.

Even though it's only been, like,
six months since the retreat,
someone on WhatsApp
suggested we all meet up,
and now it's happening, a little get-together
while the weather's nice and before we
have to go back to school in September.

It's about halfway through
the summer holidays and Cambridge,
it was agreed by everyone in the group chat,
was a good location for most people to get to
and is apparently a nice city
to hang out in and get
tasty food and stuff.

We all said it was cool
to bring a friend along –
if we wanted to –
someone who might not have been

on the retreat, for company,
but there's only one person I want to be with,
and it's the same for Leigh.
I can't wait to see Lana, of course,
and they're looking forward
to seeing Charlie.

If there's time, Leigh and I
are planning to look
around the university,
and see what the vibe is like,
because if it all goes to plan,
it won't be too long
before we might choose to apply.

Maybe, when it's the time to,
it could be Cambridge.

They've opened a new
flower shop in the station
where a pub used to be.
It's called **WILD EAST**.

I dash in quickly and buy
a bunch of white roses –
MK Dons colours –
before we board the train and
find our seats.

A year ago, coming to a new city,
starting a new school, going into

the start of my GCSEs
and not even having proper school shoes has
been a pretty mad journey.
But all things considered, I think
I've learned lots about myself.

A few weeks ago, me and Leigh even
started our own podcast
all about books, poetry and lyrics called:
On the Same Page with
Miss De La Mare and Ronny.
We plan to post a
new show every two weeks.

The first book we talked about
had to be *The Crossing,* and we even managed
to get Maher involved in the conversation.
It was brilliant that we got him
to tell his story
as a refugee, obviously,
which brought a new dimension
to our reading of the story.
An emotional complexity felt by many.

We're trying to read a good mix of books
from all different kinds
of authors from a range of
different backgrounds,
with interesting stories to tell.

Miss De La Mare and I are
not experts in literature or anything

and we've only done a few episodes so far
but we want to bring a new energy
about books that some younger
readers might not get
from their English lessons yet.

We also read this other book
called **Ugly Dogs Don't Cry**,
– which is a more modern version of
Of Mice and Men – by
DD Armstrong, which was really cool,
because you can recognize some
of the characters from the original,
even though it's set in West London.

Next week we're reading **Heartstopper**
by Alice Oseman
and then **Striking Out**
by Ian Wright and Musa Okwonga.

School, my music, the podcast,
soon to be a big brother, Lana,
the future looks golden heading
towards Cambridge, going through Ely,
with the sun shining bright and Leigh
sitting beside me buzzing to see Charlie,
me gassed to see Lana, and also
have a look around the university,
fizzing with excitement for what
**wonderfully wild things next year has in store
~~for me~~ for us all**.

READING LIST

The Black Flamingo – Dean Atta

The Crossing – Manjeet Mann

Ugly Dogs Don't Cry – DD Armstrong

Heartstopper – Alice Oseman

Striking Out – Ian Wright and Musa Okwonga

ACKNOWLEDGEMENTS

Firstly, a huge thank you to students I worked with at HLP: Commerce House, Hethersett Academy and Skinners' Academy (Hackney) for inspiring me endlessly in the writing of *Wild East*. It was immensely humbling to be so warmly welcomed in each of these spaces and have the privilege of sharing the power of creative writing with you all. Don't ever stop writing.

A special shout out to the teachers, teaching assistants, support staff, admin team and the whole wider school community in each of these settings for offering these talented young people the opportunity, in these toughest of times, to be their best selves in person and on the page. I continue to be immensely encouraged by every young person I am lucky enough to teach, present to or facilitate creatively. This book has been written for every single one of you.

I am grateful to the whole team at First Story, the wonderful creative writing charity who I first worked with in 2015, and have worked for as a writer-in-residence since 2020. Special mention to Emma Leahy, Antonia Byatt, Beth Goddard and Lusungu Chikamata especially.

Thank you to Arvon and the National Literacy Trust, who have both given me the opportunity to teach in a wide range of settings down the years. I am a better teacher, person really, because of it. My visit to Arvon's The Hurst in Shropshire, in the summer of 2021, was an experience that actually provided the seed of this story that would go on to grow and become *Wild East*.

I am tremendously lucky to have the most talented and coolest younger brother, Tyler Lovence, who is the creative mastermind, or inspired, many of Ronny's original songs in this book. Thank you always, bro.

I am thankful to Lenka Della-Porta for helping me bring *Wild East* to life visually with beautiful illustrations in the early days. And to Camilla Ru, for the striking illustrations that have since made this book complete in the most perfect way.

I am grateful to Deborah Blake for having an early look and helping me believe that this was a project with legs.

The music of Frankie Stew and Harvey Gunn continues to inspire both my own and Ronny's passion for music and words, thank you.

A whole lot of gratitude to my editor Katie Sinfield, for being thorough, wise and kind. I think Ronny may have turned you into a poet or rapper. A good one too!

It's been a dream come true really to work with the whole wonderful team at Penguin Random House: Tom Rawlinson, Philippa Neville, Mary O'Riordan, Lucy Cooper, Jenni Davis, Shreeta Shah, Katy Finch, Mandy Norman, Michelle Nathan, Harriet Venn and Nina Douglas.

Of course, none of this would be possible without my loving and supportive family. Love you all, always.

All my supportive friends, especially David Rank and Nicolas Padamsee, for either having a read of a draft or discussing possible ideas with me to make this book as good as it can be.

All my love, always, to Elisabeth. The best teacher I know. Someone who pushes me to be the best writer I can. The best person I can be.

Love you always, Zadie. I hope you like this too (when you're old enough to read it).

Not forgetting my super supportive agent, one of the best in the business, Philippa Sitters. Thank you for always having my back.

RIP Nass. RIP J. RIP all the young men taken too soon. Gone but never forgotten.

Lastly, a message of hope: always remember that your words, your voice, your story really matter. Have belief, chase those dreams.

ABOUT THE AUTHOR

Ashley Hickson-Lovence is a novelist, poet, literary critic, and lecturer of creative writing.

Wild East is his first YA verse-novel, and was partly inspired by his time as a secondary school English teacher, his own move from London to Norwich, and tutoring a group of asylum seekers at an Arvon retreat. *Wild East* also weaves in Ashley's love of British hip hop.

Ashley has written two adult novels, *The 392*, and *Your Show*, which was longlisted for the Gordon Burn Prize and shortlisted for the East Anglian Book Awards.

@AHicksonLovence